Distant Harmony

Distant Harmony

Stories from around the World

Abdus Sattar

Cover design and illustration: Tajul Imam, New York, USA
Editor: Dr. Peggy Ruff

iUniverse, Inc.
Bloomington

Distant Harmony
Stories from around the World
Copyright © 2012 by Abdus Sattar

iUniverse books may be ordered through booksellers or by contacting:

iUniverse
1663 Liberty Drive
Bloomington, IN 47403
www.iuniverse.com
1-800-Authors (1-800-288-4677)

ISBN: 978-1-4759-6487-5 (sc)
ISBN: 978-1-4759-6489-9 (e)
ISBN: 978-1-4759-6488-2 (dj)

Library of Congress Control Number: 2012922657

Printed in the United States of America

iUniverse rev. date: 2/07/2013

*For my wife, Brenda, who gives me
inspiration to follow my dreams.
For my brother Shahid Jahangir, who took me
to elementary school on his bicycle.*

The narrator of these tales journeys through time and space, fulfilling his own creative quest. Through his captivating voice and vision, Abdus Sattar transforms the disharmony of distant places into a rich melody, textured with strains of faraway wars, familial tragedy, yet always overpowering love.

—Brenda Hudson

As a gracious host, Mr. Sattar invites us into the home of his mind, his memories, and his imaginings. You will see distant lands, smell exotic scents, and bridge cultural divides through a humanity that's universal. In his stories, Abdus both exercises the soul and slakes the thirst of the poet in all of us. He is a compassionate warrior who wields the pen as his sword. Join him in these collected writings!

—Douglas Cure

Contents

Foreword

I had no clue that my first encounter with Abdus Sattar would so enrich my life. After an honors luncheon at the university where we both work, I was struggling to haul heavy boxes of dishes downstairs to my car. I knew Abdus by sight but had never officially met him. That day, in his gentlemanly way, he offered assistance. I quickly accepted, handing over the boxes to him even before introducing myself. He asked what I taught, and with the words "English and literature courses," his eyes widened. After the trek to my car, I said, "I'm so glad to finally meet you, Abdus, and thanks again. Now I owe you one!"

In his self-effacing way, Abdus asked haltingly, "Could you possibly take a little time to read a story I wrote?"

Used to such requests, I answered, "Of course." Little did I know that my limited ideas of creative writing and "good" literature were about to be exploded.

Steeped in my doctoral studies at the time, I knew all about postcolonialism and postmodern literature—at least theoretically. Here, however, right before me, were real-life examples from a real person—someone I knew, someone who had asked for my writing advice. Yet he became my teacher and I his avid student, as I savored story after story, always astounded by the beauty, poignancy, tragedy, and hope expressed by this non-native English speaker and writer.

Abdus Sattar's stories portray cruel feudal lords, legacies of colonialism, as well as fluidity of movement in time and space, a dead giveaway of postmodern writing. Yet he knew nothing of these literary critical theories. Instead, he had lived them, fleshing them out in his own powerful prose or, rather, his poetry. His stories do not merely tell; they sing. Throughout

Distant Harmony, the words of the old Bedouin in "On the Euphrates" become a refrain: "Speak to me of the glory of your heart. Let us sing the song of remembrance."

Songs of remembrance resonate from the continents of Africa, Asia, and Europe and come back to the United States, where the narrator has settled. Although he knows the riches of his adopted country, he longs for his beloved Bangladesh, where his "heartbeats mingle with the pulse of the earth." Along with the narrator of each beautifully rendered story, readers journey from continent to continent, finding beauty in all of nature and every example of humanity. Although tales of poverty, grief, loss, and hunger are sung throughout disparate cultures and diverse peoples, the refrain always riffs with a deep love of humanity and unquenchable dignity of the human spirit.

In "Glory of the Dust," the narrator reveals the source of his beliefs: "For all of us, life is a gift to be revered as divine … My mother's lessons of the oneness of living things taught me to love nature and humanity, to find strength there. That strength remained in me today."

This divine gift resounds throughout Abdus Sattar's poetic prose. With stunning language, the writer harmonizes distant melodies of political oppression, poverty, tragic loss, regret, and longing, yet always tempered with love and hope. "The Price of Freedom" ends with such an image: "Somewhere, off in the distance, a mother kingfisher watches over her newly laid eggs."

From that first story shared with me through the culmination of *Distant Harmony*, I want to thank you, Abdus, for showing me what true literature can be.

Peggy Ruff, PhD
Chair of English and Literature
Distinguished Honors Professor
Dallas, Texas

Preface

The introduction of *Distant Harmony* permits a broadening in scope, offering wider literary coverage in the fields of psychology, history, and biography, subjects that do not lend themselves to a typical synopsis format.

I have tried to create and keep alive stories people want to hear, imaginative events depicted in fiction, philosophy, and human life from around the world.

Most assertions in this book are based on true events. Occasionally, though, recalling events of forty years ago becomes a problem; survivors' recollection fails or is at odds with others' memories. Descriptions of characters, places, weather, and clothes are based on testimony from survivors, eyewitnesses, and published sources, including my own experience and literal expression.

In a fresh and cohesive collection, *Distant Harmony* calls for all of us to examine our lives and how we are connected to our past, to nature, and to our fellow human beings.

The poignant, touching moments it records will stay with you, beckoning for you to look at the world in a different way.

It is a fable of humankind's deeply rooted passions for freedom and the survival of the race and for a faith that carries the promise of salvation with it. It is a book of pathos, humor, repulsiveness, beauty, and tragedy. It is a dark, disturbing picture of human striving and failing and an enlightening book of truth, wisdom, and hope.

Acknowledgments

My gratitude continues to grow with each passing year to my longtime friend, Dr. Peggy Ruff, a senior professor of a renowned university. She encouraged and helped me shape this book.

I am forever grateful to my friend, Douglas Cure, who analyzed the book with his eagle eye and heavenly patience and gave me vital advice—a true friend indeed!

Thanks to Dr. Ansar Ahmed for being a dear friend. He was always there for me to answer my sociological and psychological queries.

My deep gratitude goes to Tajul Imam for being the expert on the cover design and all of the other unique illustrations in the book. He truly is a fine artist.

My thanks also go to Leslie Stone Hudson and Carolyn Hudson for their continual thoughtful analysis and feedback of the book.

Thanks to my thoughtful readers Candyss Hudson, Shefali Rowshan, Morgan Cure, Shahid Jahangir, Michael Trammel, Rasha Swify, Abra Haque, Harun Rashid, Debaprosad Dulal, Ziauddin, Shahidullah Lokman, and Fred Miller, who read the book before publication and made valuable suggestions.

Continuous gratitude to my cheering section, my nieces and nephews—Babul, Azad, Manju, Shahin, Arzu, Eva, Rana, Johny, Dipu, Masum, Babu, Shiham, Jannat, and Fia—and my cousins—Iqbal, Parvin, Jesmin, Khokon, Leetu, Rubu, Sohel, Snigdha, Selim, Swapan, Asma, Suraiya, Moinuddin, Jashim, Hasnu, and Nilufer—who could not wait to hear my exotic tale.

A special loving thank-you to my wife, Brenda, who continued to survive with great grace and humor while being married to a new writer.

On the Euphrates

Few places in the desert are capable of supporting even a small community for an extended period of time. So the Bedouins of this area, with their herds of sheep, goats, and camels, migrate from one barely fertile area to another. Each place offers shelter and sustains them for a time as nature replenishes the others. In the vast arid expanse of Mount Sinai, as in the Negev and the deserts of Arabia, the tribes of the Bedouin follow a traditional way of life and maintain a pastoral culture of exceptional grace, honor, and beauty as they journey by camel from oasis to oasis.

Most of the Bedouin tribes of the Sinai descend from immigrants of the Arabian Peninsula who arrived in Sinai sometime between the fourteenth and eighteenth centuries. Today, many of Sinai's Bedouins have traded their traditional customs for the pursuits and conventions of the modern world on the banks of the Euphrates. This river originates from two major sources in the Armenian mountains and flows into the Persian Gulf. Its entire course runs 1,780 miles, more than two-thirds of which is navigable by boat. The Euphrates River has an ancient history. The city of Ur, founded at the mouth of the river, was the birthplace of Abraham and the future site of the majestic city of Babylon.

***

Najar Ali, a forty-eight-year-old Bedouin, whimpered as our chaplain carried him into the tent from the Euphrates riverside. The American attack struck the area on March 3, 2006, intending to gain control of the Iraqi insurgents. The severity and magnitude of the attack were beyond imagination. The American relief marshal dispatched investigators and relief workers. Rescue crews found the bodies of civilian victims spread all around, strewn in the sand next to their scattered belongings. There were thousands of survivors from the attack. Many lost their homes and were seriously injured. Buildings were flattened, and debris was spread everywhere. Nothing was spared—not homes, barns, or animals.

Many days had passed since the devastating attack on the Euphrates. The Bedouin man still waited, his injuries yet to be fully treated. Initially, those injuries were horrifying: a fractured skull, sheared-off limbs, compound fractures, and internal bleeding. The doctors had worked frantically with limited medication. Nevertheless, his most severe injury could not be seen. He carried his pain within his heart. Virtually everyone had lost a loved one in the attack. Hastily fashioned cemeteries overflowed with new graves.

During the attack, the blood had raced swiftly through Najar's veins as he carried a young, lifeless girl in his arms. The thought of being left alone in the world devastated him. The earthly hopes and dreams that he had once carried now faded for him. A flash of memory went through his mind: the thin, hungry face of his young girl as a little child, trying to fill her lamp with kerosene on a dark night on the Sinai Mountain. A sigh echoed through his mind.

"Oh, little girl, tell me what your life with your father writes on your face. Speak to me of the glory of your heart. Let us sing the song of remembrance."

The Bedouin's eyes wandered over the dewy haze draping the vast field of a new harvest. Slowly, the lids became heavy as feelings of love and loss lulled him into the oblivion of sleep.

Najar Ali embraced death with his own arms. His only daughter, merely fourteen years old, died pressed against his chest, dust and blood covering her garments. The young girl was laid to eternal rest down the mountain slope. Wind took the mountains in its clutches, but the lonely grave remained, etched with words proclaiming the glory of God. By midday, the desert sun burned the body. By midnight, the moonlight tried to soothe the soul. Inside the grave, the silent beauty played with angels, blessed with eternal peace where time and space no longer misted her view. The deadly bombs, the explosions, and the fires waged by ruthless man could not hurt or disturb her anymore.

***

A crisp breeze drifted across, but it was warm for a February evening, and one would almost have thought autumn had come. Mrs. Carolyn Autry had just finished her dinner when the shadow of her only son, Richard, darkened the door of her house.

Richard knocked. "Mom."

"Yes?" Carolyn replied from inside.

Carolyn entertained the thought of not opening the door, not discussing her son's intentions again, but as there was no sense in ignoring him, she rose and opened it. Richard walked in and flung himself down on the couch. A pale distress had already appeared on Carolyn's face.

Richard said quietly, "I want to talk to you, Mom."

"It seems like the time for talking is over. You ignored me by enlisting in the Marines."

"Yes, but I had a good reason."

She sighed, resigned. "Well, tell what it is."

"I intend to fight in the war in Iraq. I need to do my duty by serving my country, don't I?"

Before his mother could answer, Richard drew a folded letter from his pocket.

"What's that?" she asked.

"It's an appointment letter from the Marines."

"Has it already advanced this far? Oh no, son. No, you will not join the Marines," she protested weakly.

"Why?"

"Don't ask what I don't wish to tell you," she begged and flashed her appeal to him from her upturned face and shadowed eyes.

The words seemed to astonish and disturb Richard. "I'm more serious than you think."

"What a blind, young thing you are." She was irritated.

"I need to." He gave a sigh of discontent.

"It's a shame that we parents raise our children in such dangerous ignorance. You want to get involved in war because the politicians say it's your duty, whether their motive for fighting is a good one or not. They don't care what happens to the general hardworking public. They don't care if you get hurt or die!"

"I bear the responsibility to serve my country."

Carolyn fell into thought. *The argument shouldn't end here. I'm worried and defenseless, and I'm being pressed to say something I shouldn't reveal. I can't think any more about it. It makes me too miserable. If I break down by falling into some fearful snare, my last state would be worse than this controversial situation.*

"Richard, all the wealth and fame this world has to offer mean nothing if all my children aren't with me. I long for only one thing in heaven or on earth: to be with my children. Please understand and save yourself from the terrible fate that threatens my nightmares!"

Oh, God, I can't think of it! If my boy dies, I will surely die too, she thought.

Evening passed. The two customary gate lights at Carolyn's house were illuminated, casting a golden pool onto the driveway. Richard left the house while his mother watched his car slowly disappear under the dim streetlights. The dry autumn-like wind continued to blow.

***

Richard Autry had grown up on a farm in Pennsylvania, where farm trucks ground their gears as they rumbled down the ragged green hills. He had always dreamed of becoming a Marine, the living symbol of hope, courage, and uncommon valor. He joined the Marines right after finishing college, and he was sent to Iraq on an undisclosed mission.

At two thirty in the morning, Captain Martin began organizing his forces to launch an attack on the insurgents. One battalion was to cross the desert on foot and then proceed to a small village directly across the river. At the same time, two more battalions were to fan out in the lightly forested area to the right. As all of the forces approached the target from the west, the captain's half-dozen armored cars were to launch a head-on attack down the road. At three o'clock, as the first battalion was just beginning to get in their vehicles, mortars exploded all around, creating a fearful roar. Captain Martin, hidden behind a stone wall, fought with the enemy over a Kevlar helmet belonging to Richard Autry, who had died on the spot.

More than forty million American military men and women have served and fought to defend the freedom of our country. Final tributes are rendered to those who helped secure the blessings of liberty.

In Arlington National Cemetery, the body of Richard Autry lay in a closed casket, recently arrived from Iraq. In silent ceremony, soldiers folded the American flag in the form of a triangle, showing only the stars depicting the states of the Union against a blue background. One soldier placed the flag on top of the casket, just above the left shoulder of the deceased fighter. At the conclusion of the graveside ceremony, the pallbearers lifted the flag waist-high and held it there while one of the soldiers played "Taps" on a solitary bugle. The other soldier presented the flag to the veteran's younger sister, Robin, from a grateful nation.

With a quick, beating pulse, Robin's mind rebelled at the complex pattern of victory, honor, and finality bestowed on her brother. The impurities and earthly taints of the senseless death of her young brother stained her heart. Defying restraint, tears of sorrow streamed down her radiant cheeks, the shattering chaos of death silencing her future.

As the silver dawn broke upon the Susquehanna River, dewdrops shone like pearls on green blades and new blossoms across the hillside. Not far away, Richard's mother, lying alone on her deathbed, tried to remember the many dawns and twilights of days gone by. She now confronted her nightmares. The ultimate tragedy for a parent is to outlive a child.

***

Over the miles of sand, by the winding bank of the Euphrates, the Bedouin walked slowly. Far beyond human vision, above the clouds, his mind tried to grasp the image of his daughter in heaven. In spite of a mixture of grief and pain, he tried to hang on to hope and faith in divine fulfillment. He tried to understand the workings of the eternal seer and the mysteries of His creation.

He cried aloud, "Oh, Gracious One! Take me away from this world. Oh, Lord of heaven and earth, have mercy on me."

The gentle breeze created wondrous waves in the river as the setting sun usurped the light from the universe. Though the Bedouin had been content in his poverty, his heart was now full of pain and sorrow next to the rolling beauty of the Euphrates.

Babylon still stands, observing the ruins and destruction of a lost civilization. Equally oblivious to the broken hearts of the Bedouin and the soldier's dying mother, the Euphrates, in its ancient beauty, courses to the sea.

Shadows on the Moon

*A*manda imagined that her father might come back with a deer-drawn sleigh sweeping along the track, curling around the Hudson River, and winding toward the dark oak trees of Central Park where birds sang endlessly.

Amid the crowded buildings of Manhattan, Christmas Day was crowded with the 9/11 survivors and their families. The survivors of the terrorist attack, isolated for days, stayed indoors for the most part after the incident. Although crowded, many of the families didn't come to the gathering, thinking a sudden attack could still happen outside the safe circle of the hearth. Such tragedies were best not risked or even thought about.

Years ago, when her father shared the story of Santa Claus, unseen powers were at play. Amanda thought that only her father *understood those powers. Her father began to chant, composing a rhyme to show that he possessed Santa Claus's understanding of the workings of the world. When he sang, Amanda felt that bright, intense melodies fell from the sky and the earth began to move. Mountains trembled. Lakes spilled over their shores. After a long tale, the sky's last glow faded, the stars appeared, and she eventually fell asleep.*

On this Christmas morning, nine-year-old Amanda woke up early and peered out the window. It was still dark. The Christmas service would begin soon in the nearby Manhattan church. She dressed and put on the warm coat her father had bought her two years ago. Afterward, she attempted to reach her umbrella from the top shelf, but it fell to the ground. Her body jerked, swaying awkwardly to one side.

The girl reached out for her mother. "Mom!"

"Yes!" Susan jolted upright in her bed.

Now, Amanda, who was about to receive the explosion of her mother's anger, stayed still.

***

For the last few days, it had occurred to Susan that Amanda quite often chatted to an imaginary friend. Her worries continued to grow. Compelled by something, Susan called her daughter to her side and spoke to her. "Whenever that pain of yours gets bad, don't forget to take your medicine, and don't take away the amulet the Indian spiritual man gave you."

"Okay, Mom," Amanda responded.

A single bell chimed in the little clock on the table. Susan looked at it. It was six thirty in the morning. She opened her bedroom window. A few of her neighbors stood in view. In some haste, she took a quick shower and dressed, wrapped herself in her shawl, and, with her daughter, set off down the road for the church.

***

The forty-year-old mother had taken on the sole responsibility of raising Amanda nearly two years before when Thomas Hurst, her husband, had left her for another woman. Her world was suddenly transformed. Her new life took on a different appearance. Amanda was seven, and she held many memories of her father.

After eight years of marriage, Thomas Hurst had often come out in open hostility toward Susan. After a particularly sharp argument one day, he had rushed out of the house. Upset, Susan had entered her bedroom, locking the door behind her. From that time forward, Susan was convinced that her husband, the man she had thought was dearest to her, had betrayed her for a long time. Their dissolute way of life had worn her out. Susan, now furious, frightened, and deeply shaken, thought to go to her brother if she really needed him someday.

Susan closed her robe and walked to the window, gazing out at the mystical town before her. She prayed to the Divine Master for wisdom, not to be consoled but to console, to find hope where there is despair. Throughout her bedroom, she found reminders of her husband. She felt distressed, and her physique lacked what it once had. She walked toward the mirror and gave herself a quick check, more out of force of habit than actual vanity.

Susan felt ungrounded. The incident had left her stranded in uncertainty, despair, and sadness with her little daughter. The darkness gradually thickened. As it fell, silence deepened. From her heart arose a question, "Why me?" She was angry and pacing there alone, utterly sick at heart.

As time passed, her financial affairs became steadily worse. Falling deeper and deeper into debt, Susan gave personal notes to the mortgage company and the other usurers, asking them to reduce the interest rates of her loans. When Susan thought herself on the edge of ruin, in desperation, she took a job as a seamstress.

Her shop was in a dark building on a narrow street of Queens, crowded with garbage ripening into decay, a street full of miseries of the flesh where women jeered at her for being weak and not revengeful. The women's insults made her aware of her own sham spirituality and the futility of her life. She at last saw clearly what hypocrisy her husband's life had been, unlike the shining, hollow emperor she loved.

Occasionally, sitting on a low wooden stool in a corner of her shop, Susan would speak of her husband and daughter. "When we grew up together as neighbors in Kentucky, I meekly obeyed all of Thomas's orders and endured his punishments. I was young, but I understood his character fairly well," she told Kelly, a new coworker and one she thought would become a good friend.

"Be strong for the fate that lies ahead of you, Susan," Kelly said. "From what I know of you and what you have told me, I know you are a woman of good character. You are honest and sincere, qualities that your husband must have deemed poor and ordinary."

Kelly's statement revealed the honest outlook of a person who, like so many others, was unsure of the meaning of truth, life, and death.

Susan kept talking. "I was a country girl and had not learned to ridicule everything like Thomas, the new smart city boy of New York. In the early years of our marriage, we stood by the roadside giving out handbills demonstrating justice, equality, and a race-free society. I thought my guidance and encouragement would raise everyone to be a leader of a new society."

While Amanda was little, Susan didn't give much thought to her daughter. Susan seemed happy to watch her play and laugh. At the age of seven, Amanda tried to take charge of the house. It was plain to see the little girl was trying to be her father's complete guardian.

After handing a bath towel to her father, Amanda would ask, "Won't you have your bath, Daddy?"

"Oh, yes," her father would answer with a perpetual smile on his face.

He never considered either what care or effort was needed to bring up a child. Now, the whole duty fell upon Susan to raise a child of seven as a single parent. Almost three months after her father's departure, some days, Amanda could not have a normal conversation. She simply could not pay attention to anything. It took Susan a long time to begin to understand what was wrong, what was needed, and what to do. Some days, Amanda was tense and nervous much of the time, increasingly lonesome and unable to be friendly. The night terrors were more difficult for her to overcome.

In time, Susan took Amanda to the doctor. She had genetic testing, including tests for neurological disorders, but no clear diagnosis emerged. She paced and recited the same poem again and again because she seemed to like it.

"What was the most common behavior you noticed, Susan?" Dr. Winston asked.

"Depression. And most of the time, she is absentminded," Susan responded.

"What about social skills?"

"Sometimes she is amiable and friendly, and sometimes intensely shy."

"Poor social skills indicate some kind of disorder, in particular, a lack of what's called reciprocity—the ability to listen, to empathize, and to respond in kind."

Dr. Winston gave Amanda a small dose of antipsychotic medication. She responded to it and never showed any signs of schizophrenia. Dr. Winston finally led Susan to a preliminary diagnosis that seemed to fit, Pervasive Developmental Disorder-Not Otherwise Specified (PDD-NOS).

Dr. Winston asked Susan to come to his office to set appointments for further testing. From that time forward, Susan had to manage multiple medications, trips to the doctor, and calls to various professionals, all while planning how to find her own way and make a new life.

Sometimes, Susan wished for something powerful and sudden like a tornado to seize her and shake her into oblivion—something to take her in its clutches forever and never set her back on earth. Her resentment and frustrations vanished when Amanda was threatened. Susan felt grief for the past and grief for the future, for what may never come.

In Susan's life, there was an enduring sorrow in realizing not only that Amanda was scarred emotionally and psychologically but also that her progress might end before she developed to adulthood fully.

On her longest day, when resentment and sadness filled Susan, she still knew that no one else should take care of her little girl. She chose to have her, and she loved her. It wasn't always money or even time. It was simply that she had other things to do in their daily lives.

***

The candles remained burning while everyone departed the church. Along the way, about two miles south of their church, the street narrowed, forced between buildings into a market that was colored with flowers and loud with the flow of fountains.

Susan led her daughter to a flower shop where Amanda gathered every perfect bloom and placed them in a colorful vase for her father. She allowed Amanda to be true both to her heart and to her father.

Did all diverging parents have a sharp desire to come home? Should they not fetch their children, the ones they had abandoned?

Amanda's father had disappeared into the world's multitude. Yet Susan knew that a faint hope lingered in the little girl's heart that he might come back, but no sign existed.

Amanda wandered alone by the Christmas tree in their living room. When Susan would approach her daughter with requests for dinner or a snack, Amanda would brush her off. Susan knew her daughter's thoughts were focusing on her absentee father. Later, Amanda took the flower vase she had bought earlier for her father to her room.

The night fell, and indeed, their little house with its rich treasury stood empty.

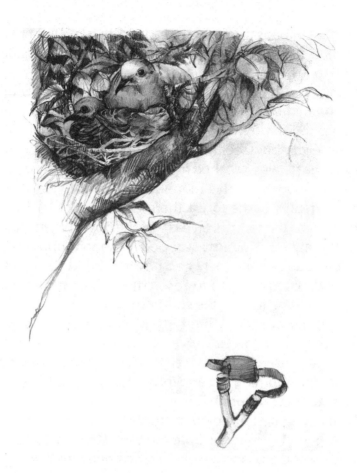

In the Mind of a Dove

Forty-five years have passed. Even now, at uncertain hours, the tale of a lonely dove returns to my heart.

I grew up in the countryside of Bangladesh. In the evenings, my mother would light our house with kerosene lanterns. The light drew mayflies, moths, and other night insects. I have often seen flowers that revealed their secrets only in the dark. The moonflower and water lilies bloom in darkness, pollinated by moths and night flies in exchange for food. Nature made the yellow primrose, found along most country roads throughout the land, to bring light to the darkness. It opens up just at dusk, so swiftly that those patient enough to take the time can see and hear it.

Many evenings in my childhood, as the sun sank, I would sit down amid clumps of these flowers and watch. I would hear a noise like popping soap bubbles, and upon looking more closely, I would see the swelling buds burst open. Before my eyes, the petals wrenched free. Shaking and twisting, they spread wide open. At this moment of twilight, there arose from the depths of the forest the most beautiful birdcall of the day. It was the sad, pensive cry of the dove. When I heard this song, my heart almost stopped. I thought about all of the expectations in life that I had never quite fulfilled. At the song's end, I lifted my head to absorb the aroma of the mango blossoms drifting in with the southern wind.

In autumn, we saw other birds flying across the sky. As the weather grew colder, we would build a fire early in the morning to stay warm. We enjoyed the companionable whisper of the burning log and its aroma, augmented by the rich oils stored up through the years of its life. Sometimes, as the heat penetrated to a hidden storehouse of the wood, the essence ignited in a sudden blue tongue of hissing flame. The cellulose, wood oils, and gases slowly turned into flame. The minerals, potash and calcium, turned to ash. Inside the ash, we would burn mothball-like bullets made of termite clay to harden them for my cousin's slingshot.

In autumn, my cousin Anu Mia used a scythe with a flint blade to cut the rice paddy at knee height. He had to pay a tribute to the landlord, either in grain or cash, according to how much land was used for cultivation and whether he owned seeds and livestock. Farmers used oxen to crush the harvested paddy under their hooves, causing the grain to separate from the chaff.

One year, the paddy grew particularly well. During the reaping and threshing of the paddy, Anu Mia joyfully bounced his little boy on the back of the ox as his wife sat on the verandah, knitting and praising their little boy's courage. All the while, doves filled the nearest courtyard, searching for grains to eat.

Anu Mia's slingshot was very important to him. He would use it to scare away the green parrots when they came to destroy his crops. The gentle doves, he left alone.

One day, my cousin let Raju, my elder brother, borrow the slingshot for a couple of days to scare off the crows that had been stealing eggs from our chicken coop. With the slingshot in hand, Raju and I crossed the groups of dwellings near the fields and along the canal. The bamboo and straw houses were arranged in rows, and only their front doors were used for light and ventilation. Behind the houses, in the green woods, a flash of gray on the branch of a tree caught our eyes. A baby dove rested with its father, I guessed. Then a second spot of gray stirred as another dove sailed on silent wings to the same branch. The mother appeared holding a morsel of food in her beak. She hopped closer to the baby. Turning eagerly, the baby lifted its crested head and hungrily accepted the food the mother poked down into its throat.

As my brother had told me to, I stopped and hid quietly behind a bush. In the lengthening shadow of a tall mango tree, my brother moved smoothly so the doves wouldn't be alarmed. From behind the bush, he raised his slingshot and took aim. The father dove fell almost thirty feet to the ground. I froze in astonishment. My heart began to pound painfully in my chest. The mother dove, together with her baby, disappeared into the thickness of the woods. I gave them my unspoken sympathy and headed back down the hill with my brother.

As time passed and the nesting season progressed, each bird established its own territory with its mate. The chirping and loud singing died down. Yet, thinking of what had happened, I simply couldn't forget about the mother dove. I contemplated her helplessness in the cruel natural world.

I wondered about the baby. I felt it had no delusion that its father would return but saw itself in its orphanhood, without a father. The baby's hope had flown away in the night, like a fleeting vision. I imagined the mother dove weeping with her spongy brown eyes holding the enormity of the world in her tears. The mournful sound coming from her beak expressed a deep sadness. I imagined that, in her fear, she heard so well that, at the slightest sound of danger, she and her baby would quickly plop to safety under a fallen leaf.

I pondered the methods of survival with which evolution has endowed earth's creatures. Did the mother dove want to build her nest in a tree on the side of a mountain covered by heavy vegetation and steep, treacherous ridges? Could she hear the quiet whoosh of the owl's wings and detect the tread of a crow's foot or the approach of an eagle? Did the mother want to hide her baby on the top branch snarled with wild thickets? In the silence of the night when nature slept and the autumn moon shone, did the mother gently rock her baby to sleep, oblivious to the weight of the woods?

I also imagined in the green forests, the rainfall of the monsoon in the morning, and the dewfall in autumn, the very spirit of the mother dove's lover, though cold in death, came back to her in dreams. In looking back at her former happiness and thinking of the days that no longer existed, her heart sank with all she had loved while her lover's soft voice echoed in her memory. At night, as the full moon's soft splendor washed over the faint, cold leaves of a world far away from hunters, the mother dove sought nothing more than a quiet home with her baby.

Did she want to be on a tree close to a spring where slippery moss and waterfall spray threatened the hunter's footing? Or did the mother dove want to be far away from the spring so the thundering stream couldn't drown out her baby's cries for help?

On the warm summer evening before departing from my home in Bangladesh to a new life, my cousins and I watched the moon rise above the bamboo groves. Leaving our shirts on the bank of the lake, we swam against the stream on the moonlit water. My cousins surfaced, and I followed. In the dusk of the moonlight, I saw them run ashore, water dripping from their young, sleek bodies, and for a fleeting moment, I understood the significant transition of my life from this young age.

The roads to the city from my village took me past many woods. As each new one appeared, the memory of my own woods reminded me of the plight of a dove. In her old age, when the mother dove's eyesight had grown dim and the wind was blowing the scent of the new harvest, I wondered if she felt the need to satisfy her hunger. Or did the scent of a new harvest bring back to her memory the loss of her loved one and being alone in the world?

After living twenty-two years in Dallas, I returned to my home in Bangladesh. I wondered if my village were still the same. Of course, it had changed considerably. After so many years, the bulldozers had taken away the mother dove's trees, her bushes, and her grasses. The boundaries of the home she and the other birds had carefully established no longer existed.

My many years of silence were a time of pondering and preparation to write about this bird's life. As a writer, I want to provide pleasure and thrills by writing stories about doves and other wildlife for the few who, no longer needing to hunt for food, fun, or excitement, can afford to put away their guns. My experience with this dove had opened up a shining vista of tales with pen and perception instead of slingshot or gun. Though I had once wanted to become a hunter, I knew I could never kill. So the doves remain my friends.

Yet the fragrance of time ascends the memory. With evening, the triumph takes the sunset hours. Beneath, a faint moon peeps from a breezy forest top, casting light upon the serene, empty, gloomy woods. My quivering, impatient soul floats in an eternal circle run by life for a lonely dove.

In Manhattan

Not long ago, on a return trip from Cyprus, I visited Shefali, one of my old friends, in Manhattan. Upon my arrival at JFK Airport in New York, she introduced me to Anita Sen, her very close friend. I anticipated a warm but short visit during my layover. However, a great gusty wind was still blowing over the airport, bringing an unprecedented cold spell with it. Because of the dreadful weather, I was forced to take refuge for the night in Manhattan, and I planned to stay with my friend.

Greeted at the stairway of her apartment by a crippled homeless man, bundled in numerous layers of shirts and sweatpants, I admitted to myself that I had a prejudice against people with physical disabilities.

"Hello, sir. How are you? My name is Mark. Can you spare a dollar? I was injured in a glass-blowing accident and lost the use of my right hand," the homeless man said.

What a compulsive talker. I reluctantly opened my wallet. After giving him a dollar bill, I entered the apartment.

The next morning, his presence, again on the stairway, disturbed me so much that I began to rave almost like a madman. Perhaps I would have been calmer if only he hadn't put his dirty hat and a beer bottle on the doorway stairs.

"Stay away from this door and find your own place," I told him.

"Sure, sir," he replied quietly. Mark stared at me blankly, took his beer bottle and hat, and silently walked away.

During my visit with my friend Shefali, we spent our time remembering the delights we had shared during college life in Bangladesh. In the evening, I made a courtesy call to Mrs. Sen, bade Shefali good-bye, and headed for Dallas, my home.

After a month or so, I received a phone call from Shefali. "Anita has arranged an interview for you with the publishing company. She pressed her prosperous former school friend to look over the bundle of your manuscripts."

In hopes that MacMillan might be willing to help me with some publishing, I immediately made plans to fly to New York.

Shefali met me at the airport and accompanied me to Anita's house. There, our hostess greeted us humbly and made us comfortable as we waited for my appointment with Mr. Godowsky of the publishing company. During my brief stay, I learned much about this kind lady and her own troubled past.

Anita was born in Barisal, Bangladesh, during the last era of British colonial rule in India. Her father, Amit Sarker, was a Hindu *zamindar*[1] of the Barisal District. Anita described her

---

1 A landlord appointed by a British colonial ruler

first interesting experiences with reading, prompted by her father.

"What would you like to read tonight, the ghost story or the poem?" her father asked one night.

"I would like to read everything, Father," she answered.

"Really? Everything?" her father asked, delighted with her thirst for knowledge.

Anita told us that she and her father sometimes spent nearly the entire night alternately reading aloud. Eventually, she discovered and eagerly read many other books in her father's collection, works that demand something from the intellect: Shakespeare, Gandhi, and Tagore, an Indian poet who won the Nobel Prize for literature.

Later in life, through her efforts, Anita had secured a position collecting land taxes for her father. This turning point of her life put her into the society of her time and made possible her growing familiarity with the politics of Hindu activists.

She then told Shefali and me about an event that revealed the political and economic strife of that time. The poor Muslim peasant Nader, a rice grower, had been brought to trial in their courtyard.

"Why didn't you pay the full taxes, Nader?" Anita's father asked fiercely.

"The rice didn't grow well this year because of the drought, my lord. The taxes in return for the cultivated land are beyond my means and seem excessive for my poor family and me." Nader paused and gazed over the wide, drought-ridden plain. "Look at the field, my lord. As far as you can see, all the farmers are gathering their thin-grown rice, anxious for their taxes. I cannot bear to lose this land that has taken all my money and strength to work and which I have loved passionately throughout my entire life."

The Muslims had tried to convince Anita's father to divide the land equally among the Muslim and Hindu peasants to avoid conflicts, but he refused the idea of equal distribution. "There is no guarantee that the Muslim peasants would be able to pay the bid without borrowing the money from me anyway."

Eventually, an uprising of the Muslim peasants befell Anita's father. During the trouble, he sought shelter with the British colonial ruler, who took advantage of his need.

The British ruler demanded, "You will collect higher taxes for the province under your jurisdiction. This will be the payment for your shelter."

Anita's father said, "I will agree to your terms and conditions."

In acquiescing, he had allied himself with the provincial British authority. To finally quell the uprising, he ordered Nader's arrest. Nader's land and house were then raided and sacked.

Anita confessed, "I exhibited my authority and strongly supported my father's decision. I arranged to take the land from Nader and gave it to a Hindu farmer for cultivation. Later, the poor peasant Nader hanged himself, and as a result, his wife Amina gave up their little one-year-old daughter for adoption to a family in Comilla."

After India's independence from British colonial rule, Anita's father migrated to Calcutta, India. Soon afterward, the Hindu society invited Anita to go to Delhi, the capital city, to convince others of the importance of Hindu dominance in India against Muslims. In Delhi, because of her racial attitude, Anita became involved in a bitter political quarrel with the Muslims and local Christians.

Also while in Delhi, Anita fell in love with Ajit Sen, an engineer working for the Tata Company in Bombay. After their marriage, Anita made a special effort to have a cheerful house and an enjoyable social life. Although her duties in politics kept them from spending much time together at home, the years in Bombay were happy ones. The birth of a son, Roy, gave her new activities and responsibilities in addition to her political engagement.

After graduating with a master's degree from the India Institute of Technology, Roy went to the United States to obtain his doctorate degree. A few years later, wishing to be near Roy, who had been diagnosed with bipolar disease, his parents eventually moved to New York.

In the spring, Roy's health declined rapidly. His career as a scientist had been extremely successful, but no promotion and fame would lessen the pain in his parents' hearts. After a beautiful summer at his parents' home, Roy died.

Anita remembered her child prolonging his school vacation period by falsifying her signature on absentee notes. "Roy gained much satisfaction when he was able to feign sickness, even to the point of convincing the family doctor that he needed glasses. The poor doctor couldn't explain," she mentioned laughingly while tapping her feet in time with the Tagore song, playing slowly from her stereo.

"How much sugar do you want?" Shefali was preparing coffee in Anita's kitchen.

"No sugar, just black," Anita replied.

"Any sugar for you, my friend?"

"Oh, yes. At least three teaspoons," I replied.

Heartbroken, Anita and her husband now resided in a senior citizens home in a Manhattan park, which stood in strong contrast to the surrounding Madison Square Garden area. A Hindu activist in her youth, Anita, in this quiet and lonely house, today believed in the divine revelation, at least in her own satisfied opinion.

"In my youth, I very often exchanged confidences with other Hindu activists on the subject of Muslim tyranny, embellishing my remarks with arbitrary childish ignorance."

Now, her confession revealed a personal account of her past passion and prejudice. She repented her past, driven by her desire to ask forgiveness from the poor peasant, Nader, in paradise.

After the tea break, we prepared to go see Mr. Godowsky in Jackson Heights. On our way, in the lonely, dark corner of a temple by the subway station, I saw Mark sitting on the hard ground. Recalling Anita's story, I felt the blood rush through my veins.

I approached Mark. "Do you remember me?"

"Yes, I do."

"I would like to ask your forgiveness for my behavior the other day."

"That wasn't your fault, sir. I rather asked forgiveness for myself from the Almighty for being in someone's doorway and inconveniencing others. In the last day of the judgment, I myself, the sinner, cannot take time from our Lord, who would come down from His throne and joyfully reward the virtuous one."

"Oh," I mumbled, somewhat ashamed and surprised by his humble insight.

We boarded the train. The wind came up as it gathered full speed toward Jackson Heights. The ripples were rampant in my heart. If I could not become the emissary of the deformed and suffering and see the supreme truth beyond time and space in its entirety, then what purpose was there in my being born?

The soft melody of Tagore's song from Mrs. Sen's stereo echoed in my ear: "My weariness, forgive me, oh my Lord."

A Desert Sketch

The legendary generosity of Arab hospitality ultimately serves the one great goal of Bedouin life and religion. Although Mariam experienced a strong sense of religious rules and obligations to family and neighbors, her life was a joyous one with her loving father. Suffering is the ransom paid by the pious, and this word can be uttered when speaking of Bedouin life. Hearing her father's name will always awaken the memory of the acquisition of knowledge in Mariam's life and the moment she realized the importance of its discovery.

Continuing to live in closely knit groups of families and tribes, in tents woven and stitched by women from the hair of family goats and camels, the Bedouins have survived the ravages of nature. The tents are usually divided into two rooms, one for greeting guests and the other for the women. For centuries, the Bedouin alone dominated the desert land. When the tribe moves, the Bedouin wife is in charge of dismantling the tent, packing it on the camel, and reassembling it at the new site. They not only control but also characterize the desert life. For those Bedouins who still choose to live in tents, the clutter of development has moved into their camps. Before the oil boom, a nomadic family's sparse belongings consisted of coffeepots, cooking utensils, and some rugs on which to sleep. The Bedouin family now possesses insulated coolers, along with other modern amenities of life.

***

While traveling toward Baghdad, the caravan stopped and camped in the north of Saudi Arabia, an extension of the Syrian Desert. After the trip of five days across the desert in the blazing sun and in the teeth of a sandstorm, they found the land looking fresh and welcoming with sparse grass, steppe vegetation for grazing camels, goats, and sheep, and extensive date palm groves for their own sustenance. Along with the other members of the group in the new land, the first night after a long day's work, Mariam and her father went to bed at sunset.

Early the next morning, before sunrise, Mariam lay awake, remaining in her bed. She watched her father wake and complete his morning prayers.

"Mariam, it is time to milk. Wake up and milk the camels," entreated Najar.

Najar usually milked the camels, but they showed a fondness for his daughter's hands. Sometimes when Najar tried to milk them, they refused to stand still, choosing only to cooperate with their favorite, Mariam. She had discovered which of the camels preferred her style and manipulated it for much better milking.

Around noon, in the midst of the vegetation, Najar stood serenely with his daughter, putting his leathery feet in *madas sharqi*[2] while his layered and flowing robes dropped down to

---

2 Traditional sandals

the ground. Oblivious to the desert heat, they stood watch over their flock of goats and sheep. They gazed over the spotty vegetation that had survived an oil explosion, one result of an onslaught of progress in Arabia. In the latter part of the evening, accompanied by his daughter, Najar was walking toward home from the field with his flock in an adjoining vale.

"Do you know, Mariam, that you are the lineal descendant of the legendarily tough and fiercely independent nomads of the Arabian Peninsula?" said Najar.

"I've never heard that before, Papa."

"Well, it's true."

"I've heard that my forefathers had seen better days before they came to Mount Sinai. They had once kept fifteen camels, and we now keep only three."

"That's right. Modern transportation has destroyed our economy. People rarely need to be transported by camel anymore. What meager cash our forefathers scraped together came from transporting goods across the deserts or selling camels."

"Camels give us milk too, Papa."

"Oh, yes, as a matter of fact, camels are the mainstay of the Bedouin tribe. They are our means of transport and commerce, and when they die, we use them for food. For their owners, they not only provide milk for food but dung for fuel and urine for hair tonic."

"Our campsite's beautiful with nature and greenery, Papa."

"We're thankful. Nature is very near to God, my child."

"Where is God? What is He like?"

"God is everywhere. His bounty is evident in all His creations you see around you. He is forgiving and merciful."

"If He is forgiving and merciful, why is there war? Why do people die in the war? Why are there so much pain, hunger, and sorrow in the world?"

"Some of God's work and mysteries are beyond human comprehension. No human pain and suffering are so deep and meaningful that the peace and the divine reason behind them cannot be seen. Keep faith in God. He is the judge. You will understand when you grow up."

"Osman, next to our tent, is sick. How can we help him and remove his pain, Papa?"

"Yes, I know. Only God can remove his pain. We can pray, show our simple and genuine devotion to God, and ask for forgiveness for him, us, and all humankind."

"Amina is taking care of her Uncle Osman."

"I'm really happy to know that. Loyalty is anchored within Bedouin families. The family cares for the divorced or widowed woman and her orphan children and so on. Not to care for family and neighbors is considered a disgrace in our religion. It should be evident in every family."

"Mr. Osman is very scared."

"I know, Mariam. We should pray for his courage."

"How can courage help him, Papa?"

"Courage is the ability to endure deprivation, withstand physical pain, or suffer emotional stress without any sign of suffering. Any sickness is God's will. God sometimes examines our faith by giving us disease and discomfort. He is the supreme one and can do anything He wants. We will go and visit Mr. Osman tomorrow."

"That will be nice. Let's go, Papa."

"We will."

While walking back home from the field with her father, Mariam occasionally gave a smart nod in confirmation of agreement with him. As they crested a sandy incline, Mariam said, "I am hungry, Papa."

Najar reached into the aluminum tin slung upon his arm buzzing with flies and pulled out a few sticky dates. "Here you go, girl."

"Thank you, Papa." Mariam gratefully took the dates, peeled their sand-coated skin, and chewed the sweet meat. "Why don't you eat some, Papa?"

"Oh no. I'm not hungry."

"Papa, you said we are going to Iraq, by the Euphrates."

"That's right."

"How will you find your way?"

"Well, we navigate by the stars, familiar landmarks, and stone marks that were left on a previous trek to point the way. Little in the desert escapes a Bedouin's eye. A Bedouin knows where and when he can find water and whether it is toxic or just brackish. The growth of shrubs tells us when it rained and how much. Signs left in the desert sand proclaim who has been there before and the size of their flocks. We are Bedouin, inhabitants of the desert. We know the desert." He changed the subject. "You milked two camels. I am very proud of you."

"Thank you, Papa."

"This is your day. I will cook you a surprise dinner."

"Oh! Really, Papa?"

"Yes, what would you like to eat?"

"Well, a lamb chop if you can get it. If you can't, black peas. And if you can't get that, then Arabian bread."

"Okay, let me see."

Upon reaching home, Mariam entered the tent and came out carrying piles of quilts and mattresses made from cotton wadding, which she rolled out on the ground by the tent so she could rest as her father had suggested. She reclined on a square bolster and extended her hand to reach the aluminum pot of dates, but no dates were in the pot.

"Oh, Papa!" She knew the surprise dinner would soon diminish her hunger, but she remained quite depressed all evening.

She was devastated at the realization that her father's story of not being hungry had been a lie, his attempt at hiding the truth from her, of hiding the poverty. No one but she seemed to see the sorrow of it. To be certain, no one knew how cruelly it touched her tender heart. Everything was quiet. Her heart sank with pain as she realized her father had given her the last of the dates. There were no more for him to eat.

In front of the tent, a campfire burned, warming a traditional teapot. Mariam lay waiting on the mattress for her surprise dinner. The outer portion of the hill on which she found herself had been left uncultivated for some time and was now dry and rank with wild bloom that sent up mists of pollen at the slightest touch. Red and purple flowers formed a polychrome as dazzling as that of flowers cultivated by an experienced gardener. The kerosene flame stretched itself tall and began jigging up and down with the gusty wind. Not a soul had passed that way for a long time. The faint sounds of Najar's cooking utensils were the only human sounds audible within the rim of the silent mountain.

The day was no more. The shadow was upon the earth. In a lonely desert, cooking for his little girl, a poor Bedouin's hope endured for a better life in Baghdad.

The Brass Pitcher

Mamadi, the young daughter of our main housekeeper during the Liberation War of Bangladesh, matured. The shiny black hair of her childhood became white with a hint of red, lightly colored by henna and bleached by the bright sun. She walked with a slight limp in her left leg while carrying the water pitcher from the nearby tube well[3] for the schoolchildren. With the heartiest hospitality and affection, she greeted little children in the driveway and

3 A type of water well in which a five-to-eight-inch-wide stainless-steel tube or pipe is bored into an underground aquifer. The lower end is fitted with a strainer, and a pump at the top lifts water for irrigation. The required depth of the well depends on the depth of the water table.

escorted them into the classroom. She spoke in local phrases with her unique Comillian accent.

The Liberation War of Bangladesh was an armed conflict pitting West Pakistan against East Pakistan. As a result, East Pakistan seceded to become the independent nation of Bangladesh. The war broke out on March 26, 1971, as army units directed by West Pakistan launched a military operation against Bengali intelligentsia, armed personnel, civilians, and students, who were demanding independence. The whole of the Bengali people rebelled and formed Mukti Bahini[4] to fight against the army of West Pakistan. Finally, on December 16, 1971, the Mukti Bahini decisively defeated the West Pakistani forces deployed in East Pakistan and liberated the country as Bangladesh.

During this sudden attack, I was fleeing from Zahurul Haque Hall, my Dhaka University dormitory, to Comilla, a little town situated one hundred miles east of Dhaka. A 1962 Land Rover arrived at the gate of my dormitory with an unofficial Bengali flag whipping in the cold midnight wind. As I clambered down from the third floor, the chauffeur trotted out from the Jeep toward me.

He walked up to me, shouting over the sound of nearby firing, "Mr. Safa?"

"Yes." I grabbed at my scarf threatening to blow off in the wind, and I peered at the driver in surprise.

"The sector commander is ready to see you. Please come this way. Where is your bag?"

In answer, I gave the driver my bag. He bundled it into the back and then held the door for someone to get in. It took me a second to realize the door was being held open for me.

The driver tooted his horn as the vehicle inched its way into the midnight scene. Rickshaws and scooters were fleeing, creating traffic jams on the city streets. On the Burigonga River, the lone ferry loaded with men, women, and children

---

4 Guerrilla groups

set out for the fifteen-minute crossing. The long oars, each manned by two sturdy young men, dipped silently into the river, and the square, flat-bottomed boat moved off to the other shore.

"You have one hour to be on the other bank with your guns, ready to fight. The women and children who make the trip must take shelter in the meadows above. If for some reason you are separated, try to go to the nearest freedom-fighting camp. Cross the river. Go!" I instructed the group of freedom fighters and civilians who were ready for combat.

After helping this group, we began driving again. We reached our base in a couple hours, and I could see a few of the freedom fighters, waiting anxiously. They had nearly shredded the Pakistani flag, fluttering from a high pole in the center of the parade ground. An unofficial Bengali flag billowed atop a makeshift rod in front of the solid bungalow. A tall, dark-haired man strode quickly down the steps to greet our vehicle as the driver hopped out and again held the door open for me.

"Hello, I am Major Riz. You must be Captain Safa."

"Yes, I am."

"Welcome to Comilla." Major Riz led me through the courtyard to my bedroom.

I peered through the gate and saw a truck loaded with wooden crates parked in one corner.

The next morning, the housekeeper served breakfast for two. She entered with a *gamsa*[5] draped over one forearm and proceeded to serve us tea. I glanced around curiously.

"This is Captain Safa," Major Riz introduced me.

Avoiding my eyes, just above a whisper, the housekeeper replied, "Hello, Captain Safa. My name is Mariam."

After the introduction, Mariam scurried out with the teacups. Over cigarettes after breakfast, Major Riz got down to business. "You saw the truck out there."

5 A towel

I nodded.

He continued to explain, "It is carrying light machine guns and documents. The chief commander would like these driven down to the Noa Khali border. Once there, you will have someone to help walk the boxes through the mountain range to the Pakistani border."

"I'm ready."

"I'm glad to hear that. It will be a few more days before more trucks are ready to go to different sectors. Mamadi will show you around here."

While walking through the verandah, Mamadi, a little girl of nine, glanced up. "Do you have a gun too, Mr. Safa?"

"Why? Who else has one?"

"Mr. Riz."

"Oh. Yes, I have one too."

"Why do you carry a gun?"

"I'm a soldier. I protect people with it."

"Mama said to never touch a gun."

"A little princess like you should never touch a gun. Mama's right," I confirmed.

"But I need to touch it."

"Why do you need to touch a gun?"

"I want to catch a wild chicken with it," she stated matter-of-factly.

"Oh!"

One day, Mamadi, who her mother appointed to be a housekeeper, had been chasing a cat along the roof of the major's bungalow when she happened to look through the window and saw a big chicken on the nearby Moina Moti Hill. She immediately framed an elaborate trick to catch it by spreading a net.

I tried to show my interest, and a friendship developed between us as we worked on her plan to catch a wild chicken. From that time forward, we spent every available moment together while her mother was busy with the household work.

Mamadi's mind was inevitably drawn to the great voyages of discovery, and she would calculate for hours how and where to spread the net.

For a while, there was more talk in the small house about the peculiar arrangement of catching a wild chicken than any topic of my war plan. We shared our lives for the next nine months. I told her about school, army lives, and adventures. She told me about her life in Comilla and her dream of education and enough food in a newly liberated Bangladesh. I promised that everyone who helped and fought against these bad people was going to be safe and they all eventually would be rewarded for their work for the Mukti Bahini.

The liberation war lasted three-quarters of a year. Throughout those long months, I was rarely able to sleep for any length of time. I would listen to the wind and the occasional distant cry of a wolf from the hill. The cold crept up from the frozen earth through the flattened sleeping mats. Toward dawn, I began to blow on the coals of the fire from the night before resting in a clay bowl. The fire rose slowly and reluctantly. A diffuse red glow in the darkness, it lit my face brightly each time I blew in its direction. When the heat began to snap at the air, I laid the small handful of twigs that Mamadi had collected from the nearby woods, out of her kindness to me, upon the fire.

***

After twenty-eight years, on December 16, 1999, the survivors of the Fourteenth Platoon of the liberation war entered the city of Comilla for a reunion and celebration of Bangladesh's Independence Day. A few miles outside the city, I found a gate made from a banana tree welcoming the surviving members of the Fourteenth Platoon. Several government officials from Comilla were waiting for us. The officials were dressed in *mujib* coats.[6] I found the reception committee endearing. They all kept repeating that the death of Major Riz was a terrible accident and hoped I could convince the people that such was the fact behind the tragedy.

Independence Day brought various people mingling in the streets. The noble women of Comilla braided their hair with flowers and coral. Roadside vendors sold homemade cookies and peanuts from their bamboo baskets. The skins of snow leopard and tiger hung alongside Indian saris. Mounds of spices and tea were arrayed beside piles of nails and stacks of matchboxes. Tall towers of aluminum pots and brass pitchers on bullock carts from India seemed to be the most desired imports.

As I enjoyed the traditional welcome, I noticed, in the corner of the ballroom, a woman who was certainly not a guest. My eyes were drawn continually to her. Poles and other people kept her obscured while she poured water from her clay pitcher to the reservoir until I drew closer. I saw it was Mamadi.

An estimated three million people had lost their lives in the Liberation War of Bangladesh. In the postwar famine, the struggle against exhaustion and starvation were too much for Mamadi's mother. From the list of deceased civilians, I knew she had died in the relief camp.

"I would have been happy if only I had been able to feed my mother one full meal before she was gone," Mamadi said.

After her mother's death, Mamadi had been placed in an orphanage. Having grown up in such an environment, she was especially sensitive to the value of freedom and the equality of all people. Later in life, the overseers arranged a job for her, supplying water to the orphanage and the nearby elementary school.

---

6 A coat worn by the national leader of Bangladesh

The Independence Day celebration and dinner were about to begin. Along with other modern young artists, Abdul Jabber[7] visited there that evening for dinner and a concert. There were no tears, only joking and laughter. In the ballroom, just fifty yards away, someone strummed rhythmically the strings of a guitar. The music sounded like the native Indian melody of the desert at night.

"Against my better judgment," Mamadi explained, "I exhausted my personal savings to pay for the treatment of my bullet-riddled left leg, a result of the liberation war. My only remaining expense is my clay pitcher. It breaks frequently and has to be repaired or replaced."

The little girl who helped a soldier and a friend in the liberation war was never rewarded. She never had enough food, along with the many others who liberated Bangladesh, despite the promises of the leaders and government.

After twenty-eight years of independence, Mamadi still could not save enough money to buy a brass pitcher.

"I will buy you a brass pitcher," I offered. I simply wanted to make her work easier.

Instead, she chose to be resolute. "No, no. I will keep my clay pitcher."

I spread my silence over the pale evening sky. It sought the voice to give value to the goodness of Mamadi's existence. From that time forward, beyond the vast emancipated life, equality, pain, and sorrows, I found her beauty ever more plainly, even more lovingly.

---

7 A famous Bangladesh vocalist

Journey of a Lonely Heart

B uilt on a mountaintop, the cottage high in the Adirondacks offered a lovely retreat for writers. The stout, tall bell towers of an ancient Anglican church watched over it. The town below, settled along the Hudson River, held a wealth of cobbled streets lined with houses, shops, and cafés. The local cuisine offered a memorable gastronomic experience rich in the northern tradition. In the summer, orchids bloomed, and clusters of brilliantly colored wildflowers danced across the valley. Wishing to be near a very dear friend for a few days and to complete some writing, I lodged in this tranquil corner of New York.

I had passed my childhood in a world separated from the Adirondack cottage by much more than just time. I grew up on the bank of another river, the Meghna, in the midst of the hungry millions of Bangladesh. One winter, I delighted in a new pair of red rubber shoes my mother bought for me. When Emperor Siraj of India paid one thousand rupees for his new pair of *nagra*[8] in 1756, I doubt he experienced as much excitement as I did with those rubber shoes. Another season, there was drought in every pond and lake. It killed my mother's homegrown cucumber vines and the vast land of crops of the poor peasants.

The days passed, and the months and years rolled by. I grew up in this poverty-stricken country, dreaming of a vigorous, dazzling image of life.

I didn't know what took me abroad, perhaps the quest for knowledge or dreams of my youth. I no longer tried to measure the losses or gains of my life against what might have been. Here in the United States of America, my heartbeat became fainter and less intense, and I could admit that freely. This country provided opportunities and wonders. The Painter had decorated its surface carefully with many colors, and I found myself sinking in the confluence of these colors and cultures. The gap between my progress and my family expectations became wider day by day. Sadness, failure, and fear bore heavily upon me.

As time passed, I renewed my dream, that dazzling, vigorous image reformed. In search of happiness, I crossed the Mississippi River and traveled through the Smoky Mountains of Tennessee. I saw the cotton-soft snow on the mountaintops of Kentucky. Northward to New York, at the tombstone of Mark Twain, I experienced historic and literary charm. Yet nothing quenched my thirst. My spirit wanted to return to the silver dawn in the green forest of Bangladesh. It wanted to go back

---

8 Traditional Indian shoes

to the hungry hours with Shukon Ali, my childhood playmate. I wanted to touch the poor peasant's golden years.

While reflecting in the comfort of my New York cottage, my mind drifted back to my dear friend, whom I had come to visit. She had lost her mother just a few days prior to my arrival. Her heart was broken. It sank in the sorrowful hours and loneliness. Her soul anguished with astonishing pain. She nervously envisioned the serene light of paradise. She whispered nothing was important to her. No light and glory were able to touch her broken heart. I sighed her beautiful name, Isabella.

It appeared to me that she had thought to escape and become a great rose in the deep, dark forest. Her fragrance attracted me as I rode up on a white horse to save her from the dark. She sought to evade me and became a star in the sky of heaven. I came riding upon a million crimson years to pick her up.

In the cottage, my mind floated in the ethereal realm of eternal infinity, but the gusty winds of the mountaintop broke my contemplative silence. Time urged me to return to North Carolina, the home I had known for twenty-three years. I packed my belongings in a suitcase. I had to travel hundreds of miles. While driving, I passed by lakes, crossed rivers, and threaded through little towns. The hours rose up. With the sinking of the moon, dawn appeared. The earth moved forward with its kind and brutal face. On my way back to North Carolina, my mind drew back to my first home. I planned an immediate and permanent return to Bangladesh, my birthplace, where my heartbeat could once again mingle with the pulse of the earth, to the place where I first dreamed that dazzling dream of life. Now that dream had many more layers.

In my journey through life, I've accepted all of humankind, the simplicity, humility, and beauty. Before returning home, I tried to pay one last visit to my beloved friend in upstate New

York, but the urgency of my arrangements to return home kept me from taking that trip.

If you see her standing high in her luminous space or far away beyond the world's bright streams, over the ruined banks of the Hudson River, let her know I miss her. Let her know I share her sorrows. I share her pain.

The Price of Freedom

I n the deep dark of the night, the dog barked at a screech owl calling from the woodlot behind the house. A young mother, Bela, sat quietly next to the cradle of her ailing baby daughter, Eva. Bela imagined the owl as an evil spirit, and her thoughts shattered, fearing for the fate of her daughter. For the last few months, Bela's troubles had mounted. She had found herself seeking the comfort of religion and divine power.

Bela had taken the baby to Millie, a pious gray-haired lady of the village, for divine purification. As night fell, Millie lit a candle. Closing her eyes and raising her hands to the sky, she whispered, bringing the good spirit, disguised as a shepherd, from the heavens to protect and guide Bela's sickly daughter. Sitting on a mat inside a circle marked by chalk, she then freed the evil spirit by sprinkling holy water from her copper bowl on the child.

She gave Bela a piece of herbal root tied with a thread from an old blanket. "Take a clay bowl and fetch some water drawn after sunset from the south side of the pond. At night, soak that herbal root in the same clay bowl and rub it very gently on the bottom of the baby's feet to cure all of the evils. Clean your hands thoroughly. The caustic root could peel the skin right off."

"Thank you," said Bela. "How much do I owe?"

"Seven dollars and thirty-seven cents and three pounds of rice."

Bela paid for the lady's services.

The pious lady told Bela, "Bless you, my dear. I pray the good spirit from the heavens will watch over your baby."

Bela lived in Ratanpur, a little village in Bhola beside the Meghna River in Bangladesh. She had lost her parents in her early childhood, and her grandmother had raised her in poverty. On important occasions, Bela always wore a red coat that her mother left her. Wrapped in the coat, she looked like a lovely, delicate girl of great poetic sensitivity.

Bela's favorite playmate was her neighbor, Nandi. He and Bela had been drawn to each other since early childhood by an understanding that seemed to stretch back into some unremembered past. Nandi fancied her as a woman of true worldly wisdom. Though he loved Bela, Nandi wasn't permitted to marry her because his father sought a wealthier bride with a dowry, one suitable for their social status.

Nandi felt guilty after he told Bela the news because he believed he had broken her heart.

He told a friend of his guilt.

His friend declared bluntly, "You have destroyed Bela, and as a result, you will be forced to live with the guilt for the rest of your life."

Nandi didn't sleep or eat for days. When he did finally sleep, he had nightmares each night.

Eventually, after his father passed away, Nandi, who hadn't communicated with Bela for several years, decided the time had come at last to marry her. He decided to write her. He finished eight letters and left the ninth just short of completion. He wrote of his love, his loyalty, and his longing for her.

Not hearing any response from her, Nandi arrived in Bhola one day. He met Ruby, Bela's grandmother, who greeted him cordially and, knowing his journey from a distant town, arranged a visit with Bela. When he visited her, periods of silence and odd stares between the two encumbered any simple conversation of which they had once enjoyed. She already had developed an unhappy passion for him. She felt treachery. As a result, her anger burst upon Nandi.

Nandi yet protested his love for her. Bela, upon much importuning, had pity and yielded herself to him. After their marriage, Nandi and Bela dwelt in perpetual happiness. They expressed kindness and generosity to one another.

In the meantime, the Liberation War of Bangladesh had begun. The Mukti Bahini, the liberation force, had targeted the Laxmipur complex located several kilometers inside the international border across the Meghna River. A major communication post, Laxmipur connected the northern end of the Bhola district of East Pakistan to the south, opposite the Indian border.

Nandi left his home in the late autumn of 1971 to join the Mukti Bahini, hoping to lead some major operations in the war. Upon his departure, Bela gave him her gold chain with a costly pendant and begged him to sell it to provide himself with spending money. Traveling north to Laxmipur, Nandi, feeling the pendant against his chest, remembered his farewell to Bela and prayed for his safe return. After intensive new combat training, Nandi's sector commander gave the twenty-seven-year-old responsibility of the Laxmipur operation.

The battle of Laxmipur complex was fought November 21, 1971, between the Mukti Bahini, commanded by Nandi, and the Thirty-First Punjab Regiment of the West Pakistani army. It was one of several large-scale assaults that the Mukti Bahini launched against West Pakistani forces. Initially, the Mukti Bahini progressed slowly, traveling through a marshy stretch of land, peppered by intermittent Pakistani fire. However, the group closed in from the rear, undetected, under the cover of darkness.

The assault began at five in the morning, just as dawn broke. The Mukti Bahini launched a fierce offensive, catching the Pakistani defenses by surprise. Thirty-one Pakistani soldiers were killed, including Major Rizvi, the commander of the Thirty-First Punjab Regiment. After the winning battle, as the Mukti Bahini journeyed on, they came upon the ruins of an ancient Hindu temple that the Pakistani army had destroyed. While camping near the temple, Nandi, who had not seen his wife for more than a month, decided to go home before the next military operation.

The Pakistani army had been reinforced and was well prepared to run the counterinsurgency operation. The organized Pakistani army crushed the disorganized initial resistance of Bengali units, and by early December, the country was again under Pakistani control. As the insurgent activity declined, civilians returned to work, and normal trade resumed.

One night, the reinforced Pakistani army surrounded Nandi's house. The army captured him from his bedroom and took him through the village, stopping several times to announce the name of the criminal and the nature of his crime. Pakistani planners assumed that, if the political leaders were captured, the Bengali units disarmed, key civilians killed, and the rest sufficiently terrorized, no organized resistance would remain. The army executed Nandi near the bank of the river.

However, the Pakistani planners miscalculated their foes. Bengali soldiers formed the core of the armed resistance. The civilians, despite the terrorist campaign, supported the insurgency with logistics, intelligence, and volunteers for the irregular warfare. The eventual strain of combating the insurgency caused Pakistan to attack India on December 3, 1971, in a vain hope that, by defeating India, they could stop Indian support for the Mukti Bahini. This led directly to the Indo-Pak War of 1971 and the liberation of Bangladesh on December 16.

A little more than eight months after Nandi's death, Bela gave birth to her first child. Mourning her husband, she existed in a realm of suffering and mental anguish, sometimes wondering if her child had been born to bring more sorrow and poverty to the world. Bela lived between a mountain of profound love for her daughter and a chasm of suicidal thoughts. Living in a country where female chastity was a high standard held by both men and women, reinforced by fear of hell and hopes of heaven, Bela found her mind vacillating from one extreme to the other. A dark foreboding of hell gave way to a peaceful contemplation of God's infinite mercy and love.

Although no one could explain the reason for her mental state, she hid a vast secret in her life, one concerning her relationship with Nandi. Great battles of depravity and shame fought their way through her mind, and guilt occupied Bela. After her husband's death, Bela was morose, contemplating revenge most of the time. Instead of flying into a rage when opportunities arose, Bela, in a burst of magnanimity and pity, showed sympathetic understanding. She found herself locked in her own mental prison, unable to escape.

One early morning, Bela's neighbor, Lilly, was taking her daily walk. Noticing the back door of Bela's house ajar, a concerned Lilly approached the house. Without entering, she looked through the back window. At first glance, everything appeared to be normal. However, she soon saw Bela lying on the bed, weeping, with a wound in her forehead. Eva, Bela's baby daughter, had mysteriously disappeared. Bela refused to answer the neighbor's questions about the incident, raising the likelihood that she knew her attacker. Villagers soon gathered, jamming the road leading to Bela's house. The police were called. Upon their arrival, they barricaded the house and searched the crime scene for possible clues. There were no signs of forced entry or struggle. It appeared as though the perpetrator had access to the house. The crime scene held few clues, nothing that could link anyone directly to the crime. The neighbor took Bela to the Bhola hospital to receive treatment for the injury to her forehead. Before leaving for the hospital, she mentioned to the police that some personal items were missing, including a trunk, the red coat from her childhood, and the pendant she gave her husband when he first left for the war and which he had never sold but had brought home to her.

Authorities in charge of the investigation hoped to get more information once Bela returned from the hospital. They had not yet discovered a possible motive for anyone to take the baby. Police searched the house and surrounding area. Meanwhile, relatives and friends posted fliers and organized search parties. Thousands of fretful neighbors and friends combed the village, looking in ditches, ponds, and farm buildings for any sign of the missing baby. The investigators questioned the saddened villagers but discovered nothing.

The neighbors enjoyed Bela as a part of their community. Even though her neighbors and relatives didn't consider her capable of such a crime, the police hadn't eliminated her from suspicion. To them, Bela remained the prime suspect in the disappearance of her baby daughter, who was only two months old when she vanished.

Following Bela's release from the hospital, a police officer said, "You will need to appear at headquarters. We need to question you in connection with your daughter's disappearance."

Bela told him, "I am not involved in my daughter's disappearance. I am innocent of any crime. You need to find my daughter without delay."

The attorney appointed to speak for Bela in the weeks after Eva's disappearance stated, "Any suggestion that my client has harmed her daughter is ludicrous."

After a few days, a frantic phone call altered the focus of the investigation. In the search for Eva, investigators had uncovered another suspect. A neighbor stepped forward to speak of the incident on the condition of anonymity because of the ongoing investigation. She suggested they look closer at Shafi, a mentally challenged acquaintance who had been released from jail recently. Shafi considered himself disgraced and humiliated because he had proposed to Bela without his affections being reciprocated. Upon his release from jail, Shafi had threatened Bela, declaring he would deliver Eva's dead body to her unless she agreed to his proposal. This anonymous witness generated the first big break in the investigation.

Shafi became a person of interest. Although they didn't immediately arrest him, detectives felt confident they had found someone with a motive. Eventually, however, the police had to admit they couldn't find anything concrete to tie Shafi to the incident. Although the investigation was exhaustive, they lacked solid evidence against him.

Eventually, Bela broke her silence after several failed attempts to interview her, denying she had anything to do with her daughter's disappearance. Offering reasonable explanations for her injury, Bela pleaded that the focus move away from this rampant, unfounded, and inaccurate speculation. The most important task was simply to find her daughter.

Turmoil grew even greater in her life. Neighbors had many opinions about the real crime in the disappearance of Eva. Bela rightly feared that someone might speculate about Eva's disappearance and come up with a plausible theory of her guilt. She was obsessed with her innocence, plotting ways to destroy any evidence that might turn public opinion against her.

The darkness of her daughter's disappearance drove away the light from her life, while a fire of vengeance spread as if by a fierce storm in her heart. The flame was so high that the emotional eye followed it, looking for its end in vain. The least word spoken of Bela held such mystery and sadness that people had no choice but to weep hearing it.

Time, it seemed to Bela, refused to pass. In the late afternoons, she spent her time in sorrow, watching a kingfisher build her nest, digging a tunnel into the steep bank of the dried pond outside her back window. A long-tailed lizard crept into the nest on a stormy day and ate all of the eggs just moments before the kingfisher returned. When she saw the destruction, the kingfisher attacked and briefly fought with the lizard. The night grew cold, but the mother kingfisher never appeared at her home again. One morning, a few days later, some local boys picked up the bloodred feathers of the kingfisher lying at the roots of a jackfruit sapling near the pond.

Pain filled Bela's heart. She had once again witnessed the futility of life, cut short, with no chance to grow or develop. She didn't want to live in this unjust world anymore and wished to die so she could be reborn into eternal life. She spent time grieving by Nandi's grave, where one day, overburdened by fear, suspicion, loss, and sorrow, she committed suicide.

***

A few years later, the government of Bangladesh, in cooperation with the Swedish government, arrived in Ratanpur to provide aid in building a cyclone shelter for the local islanders. The government had selected and acquired Bela's land for the construction. At the beginning of the first day of the construction, the supervisor directed his workers to remove a massive piece of metal lying on the ground, wreckage from a ship that sank in a storm on the Meghna River in 1970. Well-schooled in obedience and hard labor, the workers grasped the enormous piece of metal. Sweating and straining, they pressed their considerable weight against it and succeeded in turning it over. Under this heavy metal, they discovered a buried trunk. Inside the trunk was a baby's corpse, wrapped in a red coat. The workers couldn't imagine how it had gotten there until someone mentioned Bela's missing objects from twenty-four years ago: a trunk, a red coat, and a pendant.

The tests conducted at a laboratory in Dhaka, in cooperation with the Swedish crime lab, found DNA evidence that the corpse was Eva. However, the metal residue on the skeleton confused the investigator, as there was no evidence of a gunshot wound. Finally, the examiner deduced the residue was from the pendant, which had been buried with Eva's dead body.

With the discovery of the child's body, the investigation turned from a missing person to a homicide case. Dr. Huda presented his report with new findings that doctors had overlooked twenty-four years earlier. The new findings revealed that Nandi couldn't produce children. It changed public opinion dramatically. The population of Ratanpur responded in favor of killing the bastard child, stating, "Bela should have killed this Satan that grew in her stomach earlier." Late as the death was, the villagers agreed that the hand of God had surely chosen Bela to kill her bastard daughter. Afflicted by the religious melancholy, nearly everyone in the village, rich and poor, rejoiced that the bastard was dead.

Regardless of the judgment, whether Bela killed Eva or lost Eva, here is buried a generation who lost their lives for the cause of freedom for their country. The tombstone of Bela stands as man's creative work. Beneath, it archives the history of love, life, hate, and death.

The story of Bela is one of the Pakistani army's four hundred thousand victims, raped during the Liberation War of Bangladesh.

On the bank of the Meghna River, the cyclone shelter is situated attractively in a tree-fringed meadow. Nearby, in the freshly turned soil beneath the blade of the plowman, the magpie robins search for earthworms. In the autumn, the cloying mask of the yellow mustard blooms fill the air around Bela's grave. Her tombstone stands with eternal silence so the next generation can witness the price of freedom.

Somewhere, off in the distance, a mother kingfisher watches over her newly laid eggs.

Legend of a Distant War

Ethiopia, in the horn of Africa, shares its border with Eritrea, Djibouti, Somalia, Kenya, and Sudan. They say it's the birthplace of humankind. The discovery in eastern Ethiopia of bones more than three million years old proves it is one of the oldest inhabited countries in the world. The country has a high, flat terrain that varies from six thousand to ten thousand feet above sea level, with a few mountains reaching above fifteen thousand feet. The elevation is highest just before the point of descent into the Great Rift Valley, which splits the raised ground diagonally. A number of rivers cross the plateau, most notably the Blue Nile, which flows from Lake Tana. The plateau gradually slopes down to the lowlands, with Sudan to the west and the Somali-inhabited plains to the southeast.

In 1936, the Italian fascist forces invaded and occupied Ethiopia. Emperor Haile Selassie was forced into exile to England. Five years later, British and Ethiopian forces defeated the Italians, and the emperor returned to his throne. After a period of civil unrest in 1974, a provisional administrative council of soldiers, "the Derg," seized power from the emperor. On August 22, 1975, Emperor Haile Selassie was strangled in the basement of his palace, after which Lieutenant Colonel Mengistu Haile Mariam assumed power as head of state and Derg chairperson. The Derg executed fifty-nine members of the royal family, along with ministers and generals of the emperor's government. A totalitarian style of government marked Mengistu's years in office. From 1977 to 1978, thousands of suspected enemies of the Derg were tortured and killed in a purge known as the Red Terror.

***

I looked at her. The details revealed themselves, bit by bit, as I approached the tollbooth at Dallas/Fort Worth Airport. She was immutable and still as stone. Her receding hairline, unassuming with carelessly curled hair, painted an unforgettable image on my mind. Her fine-featured face, neither friendly nor unfriendly, seemed focused elsewhere, like a lonely heart.

"Hello there," I said.

She did not reply. She answered my greetings with a slow and professional smile that she had mastered.

I took a courteous departure, even though my thoughts beckoned me to stay.

***

The woman, Hirut, was from Ethiopia. The Derg had held her father prisoner and murdered him during the Red Terror. She and her mother had had the good fortune to escape to the United States. Their journey took more than two months. On the night of their escape, it was pitch-black. As the enemy approached, Hirut and her mother scurried from their house to the cornfield. They hid by the marsh and saw the flames flaring out of their own burning hut, as well as the huts of the other villagers. Hirut still remembered how she sat in one particularly dark corner, waving her lantern around to keep the shadows at bay. The night wind whispered in the cornhusks. The ruthlessness of the enemy bestowed upon her a burden of chilling fear as the world spun around her, completely destroying her home.

Nearly thirty thousand refugees passed through Sudan and Kenya during the Derg's era of aggression, destruction, and torture. The regime inside the country was extremely harsh and brutal, with suspicion and rivalries creating an internal warfare among the different factions. During these tumultuous times, the roads exploded with refugees of all ages. Some were in their seventies, yet had to carry huge bundles full of their life's possessions on their backs. They walked the zigzagging muddy roads along the shoreline, leaving behind their homes and a lifetime of memories. Mothers carried hungry and crying babies in their arms, pulling prams piled with their belongings. The hunger, torment, and persecution of the survivors continued even after their settlement in the refugee camps.

Hirut and her mother migrated, as refugees, to neighboring Kenya. Upon their arrival, the Red Cross office welcomed them and gave them cornmeal, which was about all they had eaten since escaping from their homeland. Half-starved, they ate voraciously. They were scheduled to stay in the refugee camp for two months before they could finally leave for the United States. Initially, the camp officials gave them some basic instruction about how to live and operate inside the camp. Later, as the camp expanded, they recruited people from the Kikuyu and Kisihi tribes to manage a wide array of routine functions. They created the office of multicultural affairs, hiring members to work temporarily with the newcomers.

As Hirut participated in this orientation program, she noticed a young Masai. His hair was red, and his earlobes were sagging halfway down to his shoulders from the weight of his hoop earrings. He wore a rust-colored, knee-length cloth, which he had knotted up over his right shoulder. He smiled at Hirut as he approached the newcomers. Hirut watched his bronze, arrow-slim body as he gingerly moved toward her, carrying a long, sharp spear. She imagined how, without any fear at all, he could conquer the whole world and save her from all of its miseries. The Masai introduced himself as a part-time volunteer worker, and Hirut's heart began to throb. She quickly looked away. The Masai, knowing he had no control over her, felt a crushing loneliness as he looked at the one who seemed close enough to steal his heart yet appeared to be miles away.

Hirut sensed him walking away, and as she heard his voice in the distance, she imagined a life she might never have. She hastened and followed after to catch another glimpse of him, but he had already moved on. Yet Hirut could still feel his silent presence and his eyes upon her. Holding an image of his face in her mind, she searched the community to locate her newfound love. Her mind imagined the deep woods of Kenya, where cedars and mahoganies soared upward for a hundred feet or more. Her mind traveled to the edge of the Indian Ocean and its tributaries where the Masai, in his childhood, must have fished and gathered fruits and nuts with his grandfather.

As the number of refugees increased, the camp authority selected its courtyard as a place for the noonday meal. One day while serving lunch, the Masai came close to Hirut, near enough to shake hands. Hirut got a funny feeling in the pit of her stomach, and her nostrils twitched. Romping excitedly, the Masai almost collided with her, and in a split second, he slid back into his original pose.

Boxed lunches and cookies were on the table. Hirut accepted the offer of lunch and cookies the Masai served. Facing north to take advantage of the view, she sat on a sandstone slab in a mixed growth of aspen and spruce, eating her snack and thinking of her unknown future. Over the swamp, she saw so many water birds. Her glances picked up the sooty-black faces of sacred ibis, eagles, duck, and quail. Everywhere, hundreds of white cranes rocketed up from the water like an explosion of water lilies.

The Masai halted, dumfounded. He raised his glasses and stared incredulously. He quietly said to himself, "Across the shade tree sits a person romantic enough to be in my dream, a young maiden whose home should be somewhere in the United States."

During her short stay in the refugee camp, the Masai gradually revealed some of the best-kept secrets of Hirut. He learned what grains Hirut needed for nutrition to raise her chickens, what sheds for their shelter, and what materials she must have for nest building to carry them to town for selling. Hirut's discoveries of previously unknown Masai stories also joyously satisfied her insatiable curiosity.

A few days later, there she was over the swamp, happily soaking up her first meal with the Masai, making their first all-day expedition into the vast backyard of a Kenyan refugee camp.

After nearly two months, the Masai arranged for Hirut and her mother to leave the camp for Nairobi Airport and then to continue to the United States. Hirut, the little maiden, dressed up with a yellow ribbon in her hair and a knee-length skirt adorned with the design of amaryllis belladonna, an age-old Ethiopian flower.

As Hirut and her mother caught the train for Nairobi, Hirut could see the Masai's soul aching to its core at having to say good-bye. She could tell he wanted to express his love for her, but the great passion he felt for her drowned his voice.

As the Masai returned from the train station, the camp seemed empty. Within its green recesses, gusts of wind caused the leaves to scurry about. The days came and went. Each sunrise, with its chant of crickets, would torment his heart, while the silent nights would remind him of Hirut. In his mixed emotions of lost love, he could feel her pain and sorrow as if it were his own. For the Masai, each day would start thus, riddled with small worldly activities as life continued.

The train picked up speed. The air seemed heavy with dankness and decay, mixed with the intoxicating fragrance of exotic fruits and flowers. As the train passed, on either side one could see the forest afire with a blaze of gorgeous autumn color. Aside from the vivid sugar maples, oaks, and sumac, sassafras stood with its orange and scarlet hues, mixed with the deep green of the forest not yet on fire.

Kenya is a region of dramatic contrasts and extraordinary nature, of great beauty and variety on display in its infinite landscapes. It houses a lush world of wildlife and its cycle of life, death, and regeneration, unchanged by the passage of time. From the great migratory herds of the open savannah to an abundance of bird species, from the depths of a tropical rain forest to those of the Indian Ocean teeming with fish, Kenya is a world of natural wonders. Hirut knew Kenya was such a great country that she could never discover all of its mysteries. She thought the secret of an exciting life lay not in the finding of wonders but in the search for them, with her beloved Masai.

In the evening, the plane departed from the Nairobi airport. Flying was another new experience for Hirut. As the plane flew over the Pacific Ocean and approached the North American continent, black clouds covered the skies. After a short while, the clouds and gusty wind abated, and the sun appeared faintly in the western evening sky. Beneath it, the lights of Dallas appeared. By the time they landed, Hirut was visualizing a life of extraordinary abundance, peace, and beauty in the United States of America.

Together, Hirut and her mother found a small house near Grapevine Lake. They began life there existing on simple fare. As part of his routine work, a refugee camp manager occasionally came and visited the family. Hirut slept on a cot and relished her two daily meals, mainly of rice and fried beans. Hirut was a farmer's daughter, who had grown up raising chickens, ducks, and cows and had been educated in a three-room school building. There had been no television or noise of passing automobiles to disturb her quiet village life. Here, in the United States, however, she had to live with distractions of all kinds. In the dark of the night, she would awaken and wander throughout the house, often wanting to bash her head against the wall to drive out the competing noises. She felt it would be better to end this life by drowning or poisoning herself.

Hirut found a job at the tollbooth of the Dallas/Fort Worth Airport. She began working as a volunteer with local foster children. A local magazine lavished praise on her, calling her the "Angel from Africa." The community saw the incredible vitality and warmth that exuded from her beautiful eyes, and her heart appeared to them like a diamond that sparkled with noble beams. Hirut dedicated her life to the service of humanity. She wasn't content merely feeding the hungry on her limited income. She also prayed with and for the troubled children.

As time passed, life reawakened its promise of renewal and growth. As each day started anew, Hirut wondered what it would bring. Though, by the end of the day, she always found herself recalling her time in Ethiopia. She could hear the cooing of the doves from the vast coffee farm below the mountain that stretched as far as the human eye could see. Her soul would travel back and forth from the darkness of worldly confusion to the blissful light of love in the dung-plastered hut of a Masai. Her mind would wander, along with the colored sunset of Kenya, as the summer sun would dry up every pond and lake, kill the crops, and wilt the fig trees. In the spring, the torrential rains would swell the same ponds and lakes, ripping the banks of the Indian Ocean with brutal fury, only to fling its turbid waters across hundreds of miles, drowning crops and livestock and obliterating everything that stood in its way. At the end of such a day, Hirut recalled that other life so vividly that she could almost hear the fading voice of her father saying, "Oh, Hirut, hurry and bring the cattle home."

Hirut looked across the tollbooth window into the distant horizon of Dallas, and her eyes glowed in the twilight with hope for a new dawn—a dawn that wasn't to come, for she never returned to her African home.

The Glory of the Dust

For all of us, life is a gift to be revered as divine.

After recovering from critical cancer surgery, I returned home with my wife. I thought she looked like an angel to me and imagined her wings flashing brightly. After we were settled at home, she sat by my bedside. The dim light glinted in her hair. We were both frightened at the prospect of not knowing what was to come next. I saw through spiritual eyes the serene, nervous pulse of a spirit—still a woman, my love and my hope on earth.

Through the bedroom window, I could see the fully grown tulips in our garden. Spring had once again captured the world. Buds, the reassurance of new life, crowded the garden. Beyond it, I looked at the sky, and it seemed to me that I had never before appreciated the miracle of life. I perceived, somewhere in the distance, a shadowy hazel grove and fireflies rising from the greenness of the grass to praise heaven. Heaven, I saw, was arched over the entire earth and an infinite tranquility existed in its depths. I knew then that I had not seen the world before as it really was. I realized the beauty of the earth lies not in its sheen and color but beneath the surface, in its rhythm order and meaning. My mind wandered back through my memories, demonstrating to me how everything in my life was tied together to bring me to this point.

As a child, I had spent happy months in a small house in Bangladesh with my mother. In the evening, I would go out and climb to a point in the forest by the brook and watch the sun set on the autumn foliage. During those times, in the valley below, I often heard one of the shepherds play sad, lonely notes on a bamboo flute. Sitting there, listening to the melancholy tunes with the sun sinking in the twilight glow, I had a feeling of happy isolation in the incredible solitude. After the sun had disappeared, I would return home where my mother would quiz me on my homework. She used my school lessons to explain the fellowship between everything that flies, runs, or creeps upon the earth. My mother's lessons of the oneness of living things taught me to love nature and humanity, to find strength there. That strength has remained in me today.

Recalling our times together, I had fleeting memories of my mother's image. I remembered her long, white hair and the faint outline of her beauty, unblemished by the labor of raising five children in rural Bangladesh. I remembered the sweet treats my mother used to prepare on Eid Day from rice and lentils, steamed, buttered, and sugared. We treasured the gift of such delights.

Our little village was a collection of huts and tin houses packed into a small area of land. Although crowded with fifty thousand residents, the village held few opportunities for education, transportation, or entertainment. The epitome of prosperity meant that you owned a piece of land, a tea stall, or a few cows or water buffalos. The cycles of the monsoon dictated life in the village. Annual flooding from Assam, India, gave way to a season of drought, and these formed the basis of farm and village life. During the last season of the year, all of the farmers rushed to harvest the crops before the next flood. In the courtyard of our property, my mother supervised and helped prepare the recently harvested produce for consumption now and preservation for future meals.

Together with our two uncles, we raised fish in our common pond. Being the eldest of her sisters and well reputed for her kindness, my mother would help gut the fish caught in the net and divide them among our three families. Because my mother divided the fish, I wasn't allowed to pick the first stack. My cousin Hosna would appear, carrying a heavy sack to pick up her family's fish. She always picked the stack containing the fishtail, which I coveted. Even though my cousin knew I desired the fishtail, she never acknowledged it. I felt jealous that she consistently was allowed to choose first, so I would complain to myself in long, dramatic monologues and label Hosna as my selfish cousin.

Causing considerable concern among my aunts, I once quarreled with Hosna, accusing her of too much self-interest. My mother felt angered and called my cousin and me in for questioning. Although Hosna was declared innocent, my cousin's lack of sympathy or compassion over my plight angered me. After being told I was wrong about this situation, I couldn't express this anger to anyone. Out of strict respect and obedience to my mother and aunts, I had to keep the desire for fishtail to myself. My mother always silenced my complaints that I never had the opportunity to be first to pick the stack of fish. She treated me with great affection and showed her love to me but denied me any opportunity for revenge toward my cousin.

My mother's fairness extended to the entire village, not just to me. Her compassionate nature was why she deplored acts of cruelty. She often expressed her disapproval of many generally accepted practices, such as feeding the servants poor-quality food, overloading the bullock cart, or keeping pigeons as pets while eating their chicks as a delicate meal. She held a visionary and holistic view, more spiritual than most of the people around us. She bridged the gap among all kinds of people with her merciful nature.

Even though I didn't speak to my cousin often, her generosity moved me on occasion, although I would never admit it. While walking back from school, we had to pass the cemetery through an uncultivated hilly countryside. Hosna used to carry my books so we could walk faster because the cemetery reminded her of ghosts. One day, she took me to see the hut of a beggar man, whom many people believed to be crazy, but he was nothing more than a harmless old man.

While we were exploring the hut from the outside, a strong wind came up, and we found it impossible to get out of its path, so we took refuge in the hut. Seeing the beggar man in his ragged clothes, I felt terrified and started screaming.

My cousin held me tight in her arms, assuring me, "He will not hurt us."

My fear gave way to acceptance as we listened to the beggar man telling us about recent happenings in his life. He gave us some roasted peas and led us back toward our home. Hosna and I ate the peas beside the bamboo grove near the brook.

The tidal wave hit the coast of Bangladesh at midnight on November 12, 1970. On that stormy night, we were warned that the river was rising. A terrified group of villagers who had taken refuge in my cousin's darkened house planned to climb up to the roof before the house flooded. Before their objective was completed, the flood washed away many of the villagers. Along with many others, my Uncle Idris was among the missing and, sadly, was never found. After my uncle's death, my cousin Hosna's stable, young life was quickly shattered, leaving her quite unsettled. Faced with financial ruin and her family's loss of their land, Hosna's stepmother Sophia didn't know what to do. She blamed Hosna for all of these misfortunes, calling her an unlucky girl. Spurred by these beliefs, Sophia had Hosna tortured in hopes of hearing her cries for mercy. Hosna, however, remained strong and refused to show any sign of pain.

Later in life, after her husband's death, Hosna, along with her young daughter Mala, became a boarder at her childhood home. After a highly emotional reunion with Sophia, my cousin finally rescued herself from her stepmother's violence. With the passage of time, Sophia was powerfully moved to compassion and acquired the desire to do the right thing. Touched by conscience, she sought out her stepdaughter during a series of post-supper conversations where morality was the main topic of discussion.

Sophia treated Mala as a child of virtue and imaginatively impressed on her mind that she was probably destined for heaven, a stark contrast to the way she had treated her mother years before.

Hosna, now forty-five, a widow, and mother of an adorable daughter, had survived her unhappy childhood. As time passed, Sophia was unable to do the household work and sank into inactivity and despair. Soon after, she fell ill. Hosna nursed her back to health and never left her side until her death.

In her hard childhood years, the warmth of my mother sustained Hosna during their long visits together. My mother lifted her spirits by loving and praising her, which improved some of Hosna's reckless and rebellious tendencies. My mother sensed my cousin's disguised independent spirit and gave her guidance and affection. My mother's affection gave Hosna hope for the future.

Hosna may not have been without misgivings, but she cherished the appearance of grace. In later years, she expressed her guilt in choosing the first stack of fish. She lacked the ability to take joy in her feats because of the remorse she felt for having hurt me in the process. She mentioned that she didn't take the fish I wanted through her own initiative but only in response to her duty, thinking it might be the bigger stack, which would please her stepmother.

During the last stage of her life, Hosna apportioned her meager savings, designating some for her daughter and some for me. Under the arch of life, where poverty, hate, and torture surrounded her soul, I saw beauty enthroned in her heart.

As I contemplated the past, an idea struck me. My wife's love in times of my pain and sorrows, my mother's education in my life, and my cousin's faults and virtues gave me a fresh new vision with which to see the world.

All desire the luxuries of life, but what comes of them? Think of the historical loveliness of decaying ruins, the wealth of an ancient king. For humankind, with all of our virtues and faults, the neglected and unwanted things of life, even a fleck of dust on the earth, would be a rare treasure when the rhythm of life comes to an end.

One day, I saw my cousin, like a full moon, grow pale on the far horizon and disappear in the morning light. I wandered alone over the seashore, seeing the beauty that had taken form in the glory of the dust.

The Repentance

After having waged a successful liberation war against a post-colonial state, Bangladesh became a nation-state in 1971. The nine-month-long liberation war in East Pakistan, now known as Bangladesh, drew world attention because of the genocide committed by West Pakistan. It had resulted in the killing of approximately three million people and the raping of nearly four hundred thousand women. Ten million Bengalis reportedly took refuge in India to avoid the massacre by the West Pakistani army, and thirty million people were displaced within the country.

***

Throughout the small town of Roy Bazar, Dhaka, many people had encountered an old man, Benjir, who often sat by the burial ground of the war victims. This man had many different names and guises, and the tales told about him were as many as the footsteps of his journey from Dhaka to a city far outside Bangladesh.

It was often said the old man had the gift of second sight. He could tell the stories of the bodies lying in the cemetery, bring news of good fortune, or divine the hiding place of buried treasure. Some accounts painted him as a vagabond with a suitcase perpetually in his hand. People saw him spending nights around the cemetery sleeping, praying in a mosque, taking a bath in the pond, or standing on the riverside where the dead seashells lay bleaching in the sun.

A black-bearded young man named Lokman traveled across the city to meet this man. Lokman had heard tales of the old man's power and rumors that he sang things into being. Also, he had heard them say the man spoke with the dead and could tell their stories. Lokman had come to examine the man's power. While being questioned by Lokman, the old man's far-sighted eyes glanced toward the cemetery located a few yards ahead of him. The old man patiently listened to Lokman without speaking.

Lokman felt rejected. He became angry, and his voice grew louder. In his arrogance, Lokman demanded, "Tell me what you know about the cemetery. Speak of more profound matters about those who lie within."

"I came ashore to tell a tale of crime, shame, and punishment," the old man said.

"My crime was monstrous, and it offended both humanity and heaven. I encountered the tortured souls of Munir Chowdhury, Jahir Rayhan, G.C. Dev, and others who once occupied the intellectual circle of the country. I traveled a long way to redeem my sins by asking for forgiveness from them, and I also prayed for their souls."

Then abruptly, he ceased his narrative and was bound in prayer as the *azan*[9] was chanted from a nearby mosque. Upon hearing the words the old man had spoken, neither ordinary people nor sages could agree that he was the miserable sinner he claimed to be. Some speculated a number of these pious people were crossing the world and they were oblivious to one another as they prayed for human souls and paced out the measure of eternal peace in the heavens.

Little by little, Lokman came to like the old man because he was warm and polite and he could make anyone forget the day's toil with his stories. Lokman soon found himself feeling that he had wounded the pride of this spiritual man by being rude and questioning his modesty and dignity. This behavior had embarrassed many innocents in the crowds. Lokman decided he would apologize to the old man and ask for his forgiveness according to custom and prudence. Additionally, this visitor, whom the people held in high regard, would be invited to stay as long as he liked and to take his meals at the high table along with Lokman and his family. Smitten by the man's piousness and undeterred by his mysterious muteness, Lokman eventually asked the visitor to be his guest.

One evening, responding to his invitation, Benjir appeared at Lokman's place near the river. Lokman welcomed him, as was proper treatment for his newly arrived guest. The evening passed peacefully with interesting tales. Lokman offered his guest a new fine coat, although he feared it was a shabby present compared to the magnificent coat that Benjir deserved and likely could have afforded. At the dinner table, Benjir gave a great cry of pain and shot a look at Lokman. Then, out of cordiality, he told a chilling story. It should have remained a secret between Lokman and him. What Lokman heard when he served the guest made him drop his platter of

---

9 The Muslim call to holy prayer

roasted chicken with a crash, sending rivulets of gravy across the floor. Casting an angry and worried glance at the visitor, Lokman gazed for a moment, summoning up all of the past brutality of his race.

Lokman swore his final oath. *This man will have no mercy from me or any race on Earth. Lord, the time has come for me to take revenge for the evil that was done to my father and the country by this race during the Liberation War of Bangladesh.*

Benjir had sensed revenge in Lokman's mind. Unable to bear his brutal host's attitude, Benjir stayed no longer. He left, moving steadily up the winding river path, never rushing and never pausing along the shores of the deep lake bordering the mosque.

***

Benjir was born in 1949 in the town of Kasmir, West Pakistan, near the Indian border. The chaos of the Kasmir border dispute between India and West Pakistan drove him, his father, and his mother across Karachi, Punjab, and finally into Pindi. He was living there when the West Pakistani army was organized to attack East Pakistan, now known as Bangladesh.

When Brigadier Kasem had made a brief tour through Pindi in 1971, Benjir climbed into the high-security compound where the local intelligence was housing the Brigadier. Benjir convinced Kasem that no one would be a more loyal and grateful soldier for him, as well as for West Pakistan, than himself. Kasem, moved by the man's enthusiasm, took Benjir out of Pindi and back to Islamabad, the capital city. There, Benjir's skilled hands worked to fix broken army Jeep engines, which earned him a spot as the brigadier's mechanic and driver.

Benjir still remembered his drive forty years earlier from Pindi to Islamabad with Brigadier Kasem. Kasem liked his guns, and he was a good shot. Benjir would be driving along through the desert, and Brigadier Kasem would pull out his gun. They would be bumping up and down, and Kasem would point out a rock off in the distance.

"See that rock, Benjir?"

"Yes, I do, sir," Benjir would reply.

"Can you target it while driving?"

"Maybe."

Kasem gave Benjir the forty-five, and he shot the gun.

Bam! Benjir fired very quickly, making it look effortless. He hit the rock right in the center. He also hit the second rock that Kasem pointed out. Benjir later exhibited his detailed knowledge of all types of arms and weapons, American, Chinese, and Russian. After he impressed the brigadier with his familiarity with weapons, Benjir said he could fight his way back and retake his homeland from India if only he could secure moderate help from the government.

After the militia interviewed him in 1971 to go to East Pakistan, Benjir felt grateful to have been given a position. Moved by his work record and bravery, Brigadier Kasem awarded him a position to accompany him to East Pakistan. Benjir cooperated with Brigadier Kasem and Captain Kayum, two key officers in the West Pakistani army who coordinated the killings of teachers, doctors, and other intellectual groups in the city of Dhaka, Bangladesh.

After the first operation, Benjir sensed an overwhelming feeling by an attack of morality and low spirits, and he fled from the scene before participating in the next operation. Benjir ran for his life, fearing his commander's wrath. Disguising himself as a beggar, he left on foot, heading into the forests to hide. With fear overcoming Benjir, he continually looked behind to gauge Kasem's progress.

Benjir arrived at the doors of a mosque within an hour.

The *imam*[10] said, "You may have shelter so you won't have to move to your own place in the dark."

The imam continued, "Absolution cannot happen unless you ask for mercy from the innocent victims in whose deaths you had cooperated."

Benjir left the mosque shortly after his arrival and traveled to his own land to seek forgiveness.

Benjir experienced a difficult journey on his trip back to West Pakistan. He slept where he could find shelter, often in a mosque or on a bed of straw in the stables. At times, the balance of his body seemed broken, and the whole world around him seemed to be dying. He found devastation. Entire villages had been destroyed, and birds nested in the abandoned churches. Fields lay fallow, weed-choked, and brown because no one was left in the villages to plow them. Now, the villagers had no work to do, no place to live, and no food to eat. Famine followed plague and war. The trouble of that sad century seemed to have no limit. However, Benjir gradually adjusted to his unpleasant journey.

After he returned to West Pakistan, he asked himself once more, "Am I a soldier?" He bowed his head and uttered meekly, "I am indeed a murderer or worse than a murderer. Let me retire to a mosque and do penance for my sins."

The false hope of life blinded Benjir. When his vision was restored, he found himself alone and once more dressed in his own local Kasmir garments. Half-delirious, he contemplated the uncertainty of his unknown future. Even in his wretchedness, the strange idea of being granted absolution by asking for forgiveness from the buried souls he had helped to kill moved Benjir. From that day forward, Benjir felt remorse and penitence, and he lived as a kinder and wiser man. He eventually returned to Bangladesh for redemption.

***

10 The priest of the mosque

During the Liberation War of Bangladesh in 1971, the West Pakistani army had killed Lokman's father, along with other teachers from Dhaka University in the march of Roy Bazar. After this occurred, Lokman gave himself up to madness. The army imprisoned and tortured him; a unit of the Mukti Bahini freed him days later.

Forty years later, Lokman continued to roam near the monuments and the streets of Roy Bazar in search of all he had lost. In his madness, Lokman found a strategy for survival. He attained near-legendary status for his regular visits to the monuments in Roy Bazar. Through his indomitable presence, Lokman kept the spirit of the martyrs and the liberation war alive.

After Benjir's departure from his house, Lokman didn't see him for a week. If he thought of that scoundrel at all, it was merely to call himself a fool for letting such an enemy escape. Lokman was too shaken by rage to speak. Racked by an insatiable restlessness, he felt an urgent need to gain a kind of immortality through an act of unparalleled heroism by taking revenge on Benjir, but he never did. A few days later, onlookers found Benjir lying by the graveyard. The absence of any sign of life terrified them. No birds wheeled above the trees, and no fish leapt in the frigid waters of the nearby marsh. They only heard the whistling sound of the wind that wailed over the monuments of the martyrs, where Benjir probably had waited for his own death and nourished himself on guilt and misery.

Lokman stood out in the open cold by the monument and wondered aimlessly, *Did Benjir try to sleep in the sheltering flame of the Almighty?*

Paris to Geneva

Brook Winters, a social bon vivant of Dallas, received a letter from her friend Dominique de Bray, who lived in France. Dominique said very little about his life. He was born in Euroster, a little hilltop village in France, and was educated as an international student at the University of Texas in Austin. While in college, a few poems published in a Dallas magazine brought him an invitation to visit Harrison Winters, the magazine's editor. There, the young poet met the editor's daughter, Brook Winters. Her family had established itself well in prominent circles. She thought independently and liked the superficiality of important social characters.

Dominique was thirty when his father died suddenly, and the young man, already motherless, became the owner of his father's château and all of his wealth. After his father's death, Dominique invited Brook to visit his village and take a bike tour with him and his group from Paris to Geneva. Linking the two classic cities of Paris and Geneva, this marvelous charity cycle ride included a climb straight from the Tour de France. Cycling from the city of Paris through quiet medieval towns and famous vineyard regions, the tour group tackled the Col la Faucile, their gateway into Switzerland. Although some basic lessons and training were advisable before undertaking the challenge, one didn't need to be an athlete to enjoy the charity ride. Some people took the trip with their friends and families, but most came by themselves, a great way to make new friends and raise money for the charity.

Brook accepted her friend's offer and boarded the plane to Paris a few days before the planned event. At the airport, Dominique and his little daughter, Lorenza, who was six at the time, greeted her. At the château, after supper that evening, Brook and Dominique sat for a while in the garden. They talked about fishing, horseracing, and the simple pleasures of climbing the mountains of the region.

Dominique continued, telling her of his plans for his charity tour and dreams of personal legend. "My purpose in life is to do charity work, and after thirty years of growing up in the Euroster terrain, I know all of the cities of the region. My parents had wanted me to become a politician and, thereby, a source of pride to the family. However since I was a child, I've wanted to travel the world, and this has been much more important to me than becoming rich and famous. The thought of diminishing human suffering keeps me alive."

Listening to Dominique's stories and dreams, Brook wasn't surprised in the slightest. The evening passed, but Dominique found himself wishing it would never end, despite the fact that he knew Brook preferred the theatres and cafés of big cities. Her first taste of rural wholesomeness was vaguely unsettling.

On the first day, the journey began from Euroster to Paris, and the group had a free afternoon to explore the city.

On the second day, they biked through the province of Burgundy, where the local cuisine offered a memorable eating experience. The itinerary offered the historic winding streets of medieval settlements as the tour group set out to ride across rolling hills with oak forests, through rural France. Pedaling on, they reached Nolay, a village of fine medieval architecture, narrow streets, and timbered houses. The path then took them away from the vineyards through oak woods and prime cattle-raising countryside.

During her excursion through the town, Brook listened to a story of general helpfulness in a community of kindred spirits. One spring, when one of the villagers was sick and had disappeared, the whole village had risked death to find her. The doctor labored through dangerous drifts, and even the older priest made the trip up the snowbound mountain as they found Manta, who, having suffered for years from breast cancer, now lay dying. Facing her own situation, Brook thought how unhelpful her own soulless life had been to the needy world. As time passed, the moral and physical grandeur of her surroundings began to influence her thinking. She began to become a part of them.

On the third day, the group crossed Semur-en-Auxois. It is indisputably a beautiful town, built on a pink granite stony outcrop. The sturdy, round towers of Semur's castle guard it. The town on the Armancon River has a wealth of cobbled streets, lined with ancient houses, shops, and cafés. The significant sights in the town include the four towers, the last remains of Semur's castle, the Pont Joly[11] across the river, and the thirteenth-century Notre Dame church.

On the fourth morning, they set off in a southerly direction, just bypassing Dijon. They took their route through the wine

11 A panoramic point overlooking the medieval town of Semur-en-Auxois in France

region of Burgundy and passed through Beaune, where they crossed the Saone River. A southern rain and wind began blowing tentatively across the vineyard. The return of the red-winged blackbirds marked summer this year. Everywhere, with scarlet epaulets flashing, the blackbirds had been singing and darting about, chasing each other, shooting up like rockets, and whirling like pinwheels.

The fourth evening, the group stayed in Lons-le Saunier, a simply stunning Roman spa town. A manor-like building surrounded by thick bushes, the Hotel de Paris, where the tour group would be staying the night, finally appeared. Two concierges dressed in white, shabby jackets with wing collars came trotting from the entrance. The travelers, weary from their long bike tour, collapsed into chairs in the lobby, waiting their turn to check in at the reception desk.

"I will be handling your room keys and passports now. I will bring your bags up to your rooms in a moment," said the concierge.

As Brook climbed the stairs alongside Dominique, she said, "I'm a little surprised that the hotel appears so seedy. It has such an excellent garden outside. I just would have thought of it differently."

"The hotel is really antiquated, isn't it?"

"It is."

That evening, Dominique took Brook to a nearby restaurant.

"When the British ruled here," Dominique said, "this was a British club. Would you care for a drink?"

"Sure. I would prefer Napoleon brandy."

"Why did you come to Paris, Brook?" quizzed Dominique.

"I thought you invited me. Is there something wrong with choosing Paris?"

"No, no, just asking," said Dominique.

There is really a lot about life that is beyond comprehension, Brook thought. Many things about life could not be anticipated.

Sometimes she felt as if her life played itself out without her, unintentionally moving to the whim of some invisible power.

"Why did you join this tour?" asked Brook.

Dominique lifted his face from his wineglass. "To share something with you."

"And what might that be?" asked Brook.

Dominique discussed his rivalry with Armand Richelieu. In spite of his objections, his wife had abandoned him and Lorenza to marry Armand, a good-for-nothing who had robbed a convenience store and knifed a night clerk. Dominique now lived at the large château with his daughter, his only true happiness. He expressed his interest in the villagers by building a breast cancer center in Euroster.

Brook, wanting to encourage Dominique in his work, promised her support. Sometimes during their conversations, Dominique would reminisce about his childhood days and the girl who lived across the street from him, who would sit in front of her doorway, watching the people as they passed by. Another memory was of the same girl, dressed in yellow pajamas with paint on her face and walking about carrying a fruit basket to share with the children.

One September night, when the moon came out and the dogs began barking so loudly that everyone came to see what had happened, there was Anila. The girl had died of cancer and must now be in heaven watching the promenade of heavenly souls.

The tour group was scheduled to cross fewer miles on the fifth day, but the climb stretched long through the Jura Mountains into Switzerland. As the group left the hotel, they began climbing almost straight up from the valley. After the climb, a relaxed pace was set to enjoy the fantastic landscape and rest their legs for a while. As seen in the Tour de France, the route uphill is comprised of almost twelve kilometers of famous hairpin curves. The tour group crossed their fingers for a clear day. They were eager to set their sights on Mont Blanc. At that point, they enjoyed a great descent down to the international border, where they cruised to the finish point at Geneva.

From Switzerland, Brook planned an immediate return to the United States. Dominique had anticipated a short visit at the Geneva airport, where he bade his friend good-bye.

During the next two years, Brook became a significant financial figure in Dallas. In an attempt to support her extravagances, she worked in the real estate business, for which she was well suited. Dominique, meanwhile, kept up a busy schedule, having succeeded in turning his château into a breast cancer center.

Walking alone in the silence, Dominique had no regrets. He would have felt he lived a full life if he had died after having crossed the path from Paris to Geneva, having known the pains, joys, and sorrows of his villagers, as well as Brook's blue eyes. He felt every day was there to be lived or to mark one's departure from this world. The price of having done so might be his life, his personal legend. Now, trying to forget his love for Madeline, his wife, he buried himself in his charity work.

Brook was a fortunate woman. She was known throughout the city for her financial success. Years of wealth and easy living had made her soft, self-indulgent, and lacking public spirit. Her days were all the same, with the seemingly endless hours of work between sunrise and dusk. Brook had never imagined that she would find herself sitting in her office reflecting back over her times with Dominique. In planning her life, she had not given love much thought. The vague assumption in her subconscious mind was that time would take care of it when appropriate.

"Do I love Dominique?" she wondered aloud.

Her life with Dominique in their college years was ordinary, but by no means did she consider herself a bad friend. After returning from Geneva, with the passing of the years, an invisible link had gradually formed between them. She endured an unspeakable loneliness following her time without Dominique. Although they had been away from each other for many years, she had never considered the possibility that such a yearning could reside within the depths of her heart. At length, having returned to her house from work, Brook would often sink immediately into slumber.

One day when she awoke, Brook called Dominique to confirm the cancer center inauguration ceremony.

Dominique asked, "Will you come to the inauguration?"

"I most certainly will."

The promise slowly took on a weighty, compelling meaning for Brook.

Now, she came again to this foreign land. It was spring within the gates of a Euroster park where the cancer center stood in strong contrast to the surrounding seasonal flowers. In a distant tree, a fox sparrow sang a tinkling song of exquisite feeling. The air that had been so refreshing that morning gave way in the afternoon to a quietly pervasive heat, laden with humidity. Brook had purposely dressed herself to look elegant. She wore a black suit and tied a red ribbon in her hair. She attended to details diligently with her hands attractively manicured. When she arrived in the village, the name, Brook Cancer Center, had profoundly touched her.

Dominique found himself still passionately attracted to Brook. Finally, he asked, "Brook, will you do me the honor of being my wife?"

"Oh, Dominique, I will. I certainly will."

When Brook went to her parents to inform them of her decision to marry Dominique and move to France permanently, they, of course, were horrified.

Years later, Brook was able to say that she had lived happily in an old house with her stepdaughter Lorenza and Dominique. She had worked so responsibly as a CEO in the cancer center that she dreaded leaving her patients, even for short trips. Decades later, Dominique's effort still pulsated within the memory of countless cancer patients. Dominique and Brook immersed their lives in the charity, which single-handedly made their voice immortal to the generations of people in Euroster.

The Return

M oona, a strong and virtuous eighteen-year-old, held the eldest position of three children of a poor, hardworking family in Bhola, Bangladesh. His father was a coastal fisherman in the nearby Meghna River. Moona's father became ill after working long hours in the rain during the monsoon season. Gradually, his condition worsened, the illness became fatal, and the family income abruptly ended. Moona and his mother were forced to look for work in the village. Fortunately, Moona proved himself to be a capable handyman.

My aunt Nur Jahan was a village woman of praiseworthy character. Several of our neighbors had commended her for the kindness she showed to Moona's mother, Halima. In the time of Halima's difficulty, my aunt helped her with household jobs, such as raising water from the well, sifting the lentils, sweeping the courtyard, and chasing away the chickens from the rice paddy pile while drying it in the sun for husking. Halima had a poor record of keeping up her household, but this time, she tried to pay close attention to her job of guarding the paddy.

While Halima was busy protecting the paddy with new diligence one day, her two little girls, Jolly and Sali, approached me to play with them near the chicken coop. My mother forbade me to play with these girls, but I longed for Sali's company with the attentiveness only a young boy can display. Behind the chicken coop, Jolly opened a restaurant, serving rice and meat made of her Play-Doh. Sali and I were her customers. In Jolly's restaurant, I started crying because I didn't have any money. Sali assured me that she loved me and would let me borrow two leaves, our currency of the day. Sali taught me a rhyme that I couldn't remember exactly, but the meaning was something like "the candle burns with the oil of Bata fish." She promised to teach me more rhymes if I would come again to play with them. I wanted to learn more rhymes from Sali. I wanted to hear her assurance that she loved me, although I was fearful my mother would discover I had played in the sand with those who were forbidden. For that short time, though, Sali became my childhood playmate.

Although Moona dwelt in poverty in a broken-down house with his mother and the two girls, he still enjoyed a fine reputation in the village as an honest man and one with rare wisdom. Despite his honesty and good standing, a year after his father's death, Moona found himself a victim in his own village because of the feudal lord's displeasure.

The feudal system originated in India during British colonial rule and later expanded to Pakistan and Bangladesh. The British Empire prized indigo for the blue dye it produced, and cultivating it required the combined efforts of many well-organized farming communities under the authority of a feudal lord. In India, the British lord was at the top of the power structure. Under his jurisdiction, financial issues such as taxes, tributes, and production were powerfully managed. The lord, aided by managers, enforced his will via a network of lower functionaries. At the bottom of the social ladder was a large population comprised primarily of farmers. Although the feudal system had been abolished, its legacy of land-related exploitation continued to exist in Bangladesh.

Moona was placed in the midst of such exploitation. He soon found his house and all of his land confiscated by the feudal lord. The feudal lord had considered Moona's family members as enemies for many years because of an old boundary dispute. While the turmoil increased, Moona was forced to sell his home to the feudal lord, who offered him an unreasonably low price.

During this time of increasing difficulty, Moona and his family sought shelter with Ratan, a close relative of Halima. At Halima's suggestion, the family eventually moved to Raj Shahi, a divisional town two hundred miles away from home. With a broken heart, I said good-bye to my playmate Sali.

Ratan accompanied the family on part of their journey. As they traveled, he explained to them conditions of daily living they could expect in their new home. In Raj Shahi, Moona was a man of unknown family and origin. He had no reputation to precede him, and his appearance conveyed an effect of gloom, which corresponded to the severe and solitary disposition he now possessed. At their new home, while Moona's mother looked after Jolly and Sali, Moona wandered the town for several months doing odd jobs and supporting himself and the family as best he could.

Later, Moona moved to the countryside of Raj Shahi, where he remained for more than thirty years. There, he married a shepherd girl who bore him a son. During that time, he worked as a farmer, always hoping to save enough money to return home to Bhola, but he never found the economic situation stable enough to permit it. A wanderer in an alien land, Moona became a part of the grime and poverty of the society.

The sad routine of Moona's life came to an abrupt end many years later. One evening, day turned to night, but Moona didn't return home from work. On the way home, he had suffered a stroke, and a passerby had found him lying on the bank of the Padma River. While onlookers guarded the scene, an old woman approached, acting as though she had lost her mind. Hurrying from place to place, she searched for her son who had failed to return home from work. The woman was allowed to view the man on the riverbank, and confirming that the victim was her son, Moona's mother offered all of her small savings to take him to the nearest hospital.

At the hospital, a nurse named Julia cared for Moona. Her grace and kindness impressed him so much that, at the end of his recovery, he continued to communicate with her.

His illness reminded him of his mortality, and he became worried after a conversation with Julia. Moona decided to visit his home in Bhola while he was still able. Julia supported his decision. She thought it might relieve some of the stress of being ill. Moona's wife disagreed and urged him to delay his plans because of their financial difficulty. Submitting to his wife's wishes, Moona refrained from returning home to Bhola.

Years passed, and Moona grew older. Back in Bhola, during his last days, the feudal lord began to feel remorse for driving the Moona family into a life of poverty. The feudal lord believed that, because of his own austere manners and brooding nature, he was loved by none, hated by many, and feared by most. He realized that his life was empty and degenerate, and he felt the need to cleanse his soul before dying. Thus, the feudal lord gave up his title to the land and arranged for the Moona family and their heirs to have communal holdings in it, an act that brought him some inner peace before his death.

Almost forty-eight years after he'd left his home, Moona saw Nazir Ali, one of his childhood neighbors, at a religious gathering in Raj Shahi. Nazir told him about the decision of the dying feudal lord, who had willed his boundary-disputed estate to the Moona family. Upon learning the fabulous news, Moona determined to inquire about the property and to have one last look at his beloved homeland.

Moona sold his goat, his only prized possession, to get the money for a trip back to his village. While packing in preparation for his departure, he heard his wife screaming in another room, voicing her long-held suspicions of her husband's foolishness, which was evidenced by his desire to visit his village and spend their last wealth. Moona was shocked at her rage and nervous to undertake the trip under her disapproval, but he reasoned to himself that the steamer fare was reasonable and the financial loss wasn't severe and began preparing for his trip.

When Moona arrived in Kalikirty, the green country of Eastern Bhola, his birthplace, no one recognized him at first or acknowledged his right to be there. Eventually though, they realized who he was, and they welcomed him. This was Moona's village, where he had grown up.

Moona loved the land I love, the place where I also grew up and spent my childhood. I listened as Moona spoke of the warmth of the sun and the wind's voice in the coconut leaves. He remembered the cloying musk of the grain fields and the honest sweat of the hardworking plowmen of this village. In his own tongue, he spoke of Sona's mother, the century-old lady of the village for whom he had built rat traps in the harvesting season. He remembered Gura Mal, the *deruka*[12] hand carver, a craftsman he always wanted to emulate.

Moona vividly portrayed the men and women of the village who had lived and died. He held my attention by drawing the clarity, simplicity, humility, and beauty of our birthplace. In his childhood, Moona had gotten up early in the morning and plowed the hard soil to plant jute and rice paddy by throwing his body to the sun, wind, and rain. At last, the time came to put the paddy in the stack, the battle nuts and coconuts in the hold, and hay in the mow. With the advent of the new season, the time came again to haul away the watermelon vines that had shriveled and died after the fruit was harvested.

Moona celebrated the simple existence of life by praising all of the lives and deaths of the village. Sorrow filled his heart, but it was also full of songs about the deeply satisfying beauty of his birthplace.

Moona spent a few days in the village with my cousin, Faruk Mia.

Before Moona departed, Faruk told him, "You should go to the municipal court to obtain an application so you can claim your estate immediately on your next visit."

A delighted Moona said, "Thank you for your generosity."

Moona felt the kindness was a continuation of that shown to his family by Faruk Mia's mother, Nur Zahan, my aunt, when she helped his mother all those years ago.

After Moona experienced a long, loving farewell from the villagers, my cousin, my nephew, and I accompanied him to the river steamer station to say good-bye. He boarded the steamer, an old man of sixty-six. Through the morning fog, I saw his sad and anxious face. An astonishing pain chained my soul. In a fleeting second, my mind went riding upon a million crimson years to see the face of Moona's little sister, my childhood playmate, Sali.

---

12 A carved wooden stand for a kerosene lantern

A silent voice called out from my heart, "Oh, Moona, don't go. Oh, Sali, come home."

Slowly, leaving us behind, the steamer had already turned into the surging waves of the Tetulia River.

Prodigy

Awidow named Kamini lived in a hut on the east coast of Bangladesh. She had a fourteen-year-old daughter, Nora. At the age of fifty-four, Kamini had been married to her husband, Karamat, a woodcutter, for twenty-two years.

One day, Karamat went to cut oak in Sunder Ban. There, while working, the group of woodcutters encountered a terrifying danger. It was said, on that day, that thunderous footsteps, sounding like boulders dropping from the hills, signaled the approach of a tiger. Most woodcutters knew better than to look back, even for a glimpse. They broke into a run, with the speedy footsteps of the tiger following. Merging into an unbroken lope, it deftly kept pace with the running victims. Once they had tired, the tiger's cold clasp tightened around the neck of Karamat and dragged him to the nearest shore with irresistible force.

Following Karamat's death, no one in the village was interested in the widow Kamini and her daughter. Finally, Kamini took a job, laboring endlessly in the rice field to support her family. As she looked at Nora's face, Kamini was saddened by how hard her daughter tried to help and how terribly hungry her daughter was. Slowly, the autumn faded into winter. As the harvest ended, the rice fields were bare beneath a wintry sky that seemed to mirror Kamini's future. There would be no job until the next harvest. Without work and her husband's income, how could she go on supporting herself and her daughter? Their anxiety increased daily, and finally, after almost a year of struggling with poverty and joblessness, Kamini and Nora started begging for alms door to door.

Walking on a scenic dirt road through the country, past a long row of palm trees, which had been carefully planted to give an ornamental look, Kamini and Nora came to our house. They tried to walk quickly in order to cover a larger area, but the thick falls of her Indian sari and her age restricted Kamini's movement. Glancing at the window as she approached our house, a movement caught her eye. Through the window, she could see a face, indistinct at this distance, yet it seemed to regard her steadily. After two long years of acquaintance, she had no doubt. It must be Mrs. Rahman, my mother. Kamini was getting old.

A sweet, familiar voice eddied around the house: "God is kind." It was Kamini. She drew out her belongings and set them before her. Nora settled on a bench on the porch.

"Are you going to Katali?" my mother asked.

"No, lady mother, I don't feel good this week. Maybe next week."

"Oh! Okay."

Katali was the nearby village where my mother's little sister, my aunt, lived. Kamini once worked as a messenger for my mother whenever she traveled to Katali for alms. Occasionally, my mother would send treats with Kamini to her younger sister. Sometimes she would send homegrown green beans, cucumbers, and tomatoes.

Kamini and Nora were welcomed and fed, as was my mother's custom. She would feed the hungry whenever she could. After eating with us and receiving a handful of rice as alms, Kamini and her daughter left our house and continued traveling to the next house. I was watching as they took a turn around the cabbage field from our home. The morning was rapidly becoming afternoon. Mist began to rise and curl gently across the field from the nearby pond. Their bare feet were probably cold from it.

Nora was pretty.

"It is time for school," Mama reminded us. Our school was just across the road, where Mama could keep an eye on our behavior. Papa always made sure the children kept a few pages ahead of the rest of the class, with the hope of sending us to a good college in Dhaka with our rich cousins, Iqbal and Parveen. Soon came high school and school tuition. At twenty dollars tuition per pupil and with two children attending high school, it meant Mama needed forty dollars every month. When it was my elder brother Raju's turn for college, my mother had four hundred dollars for him to take along. Mama sent our innkeeper, Ena, a young man of twenty-two, to town with vegetables and coconuts to sell for more money. If needed, Papa would attempt to borrow some money from the *mahajon*[13] and bargain with him to wait for payment until after the next harvest.

Kamini fit smoothly into our family while begging. She had regular hours when she worked beseeching alms in our house

---

13 The village lord

and the village on Wednesday mornings. She always spoke pleasantly with us and especially with my little sister, Nadia, who was four at the time. Whenever she passed Papa, she blessed him. After some months, one Wednesday, our school was closed when Kamini came with a basket of goods to sell. Colored hair ribbons, combs, cookies, dolls, and a number of toys filled her basket. My baby sister gave a coo of recognition as her little arms reached for Kamini's face.

Throughout the years, I remembered Kamini's many attempts to get my baby sister to speak. However, neither words nor any effort meant anything to Nadia. That day, after a few more attempts, Kamini was able to teach my sister the word "Mama." It happened on the porch, where my sister was holding the doll Kamini had given to her. Kamini touched the doll's face and hair, pointed her finger to my mother's face, and kept sounding out "ma-ma."

She also helped Nadia by putting both of her hands on the face of the doll and my mother's face. It took two years of effort and herculean patience for Kamini to teach my sister to speak. Mama cried.

My mother's whimper rose to a scream, as the tears welled in her eyes. She gasped for breath, and the words died on her lips. We all stood and prayed together. Mama wanted to pay for the doll, but Kamini gave my sister the doll as a gift, as she had borrowed the whole one hundred dollars for her business from Mama, with the promise of returning it before the next semester of my brother's college.

With unabashed emotion and great natural wisdom, Mama thought neither the doctor nor the teacher should let the world of my sister be silent. She imagined the chirping of the bird and the neigh of a saddled horse. She also imagined mooing cows, the squeals of puppies, sunlight, and the quivering of soap bubbles, all the things in life that communicated without words. She thought she could bring my baby sister into contact with everything that could be reached or felt.

Kamini was so happy. The first day of her business began with a miracle. Here in the simple, unpretentious, yet profoundly joyful achievement, she wanted to spend some time with our family. Mama was delighted. She gave Kamini a pair of her old shoes after having just sewn up the loose soles earlier in town. Mama knew from now on that Kamini had to travel a lot more to sell her goods.

During her long visits, Kamini told us of her travels in the village. She knew so many things. When she told a story, it was like a ghost coming to life and marching around our room. We were scared and thrilled all at once. To carve these truths upon the minds of her audience, Kamini concocted vivid narratives of reward and punishment. This was, in part, a cunning device to hold the listeners' attention. For what commoner could resist the temptation to glimpse these wonders? Soon, it became a simple fact that we were all eager for Kamini to visit again so she could tell the rest of the tale, an exciting account of a headless ghost.

However, she never did.

One day, Kamini came home. The house seemed unnaturally quiet. In the courtyard, she paused, overcome by a chilling sensation, not uncommon in an empty house. She found her daughter on the bed, feverish, racked with pain. With her last bit of strength, Kamini ran to town to pawn her basket of goods for a minimal price. She borrowed an extra twenty-five dollars, with the promise of bringing Mr. Sikdar, the shop owner, the rice she would be collecting from alms over the next few weeks. Nora's condition remained unchanged throughout the night until a doctor came. Slowly, her shining eyes responded to the doctor's medicine. Although a wave of sickness swept over her, mercifully, she was cured. The only vestige was her mother's large debt to repay.

Time passed, and Kamini could not keep her promise to repay the loan to Mr. Sikdar.

He was furious. "That lady Kamini is a liar, a crook!"

There was also a rumor in town that Kamini had borrowed some money from another shop owner in Katali with the promise of returning it with the rice from her alms. The news was spread around the village. Mr. Sikdar shouted to all who would listen in front of his shop, breaking the village's silence. He relished in berating Kamini mercilessly. His sharp eyes appeared to see every cautious movement Kamini made. Mr. Sikdar decided to see the shop owner in Katali and to come to my mother for her signature to file a joint cheating case against Kamini in the village court.

Summer died early in the region. Kamini came to discuss her situation with my mother. While she was leaving our courtyard, Mr. Sikdar walked in and drew up beside her. He began to question her, but to his solicitous queries, she made only the faintest replies. Later, Kamini and her daughter could be seen walking briskly along, hearing little else but their own footfalls. As they reached the midpoint of their homeward walk, Mr. Sikdar's abusive screams shattered the silence. The evening lengthened as tattered clouds scuttled across the sky. Layers of fog rolled in from the river, bringing humid air with them. Beneath the mist, hares huddled in their burrows. A sickle moon cast its thin light down on palm trees. Papa came home and found Mama sitting in her rocking chair, oblivious to everything around her, seemingly in her own little world. He put out the fluttering candle Mama had lit. Its melted wax slid down the shaft in a broad stream, a winding sheet.

He looked at Mama. "Don't worry about your one hundred dollars."

Mama wept. "I didn't thank Kamini enough for the doll."

Mama had no doubts concerning the credentials of her messenger, and with instinctive sympathy, culled by her long acquaintance, she was sure she could guess what was in Kamini's mind.

This is the story of the hill country, my village, past and present, people among whom Nora and Nadia grew up and still live. My mother's soul is now at rest, as is Kamini's, whose dignity was lost in poverty, debt, and fear.

"Mama" is the only word my sister learned to speak in her entire life. Nadia, my only sister, was afflicted with autism.

About the Author

Abdus Sattar began writing while working as a senior advisor of a renowned university. He continues to work in the field of higher education. His writings describe his personal experiences and his discovery in ordinary people. He has written several short stories for magazines and community newspapers and screenplays for short films. Abdus grew up in Bangladesh. He and his wife reside in Dallas, Texas.

About the Illustrator

Many facts and fictions are brought to life in this book. Tajul's objective was to penetrate to the characters of these stories. He reveals the essence of what happened by depicting the main characters who lived through these events. His incredible murals have survived in NASA, while his other artworks are equally renowned in magazines by publishing companies and among art lovers.

My final analysis would always be the same: yes, Tajul Imam is a fine artist.